THE WEIGHT OF SNOW

ALSO BY
CHRISTIAN GUAY-POLIQUIN

Running on Fumes

Translated by Jacob Homel
Published by Talonbooks

THE WEIGHT OF SNOW

CHRISTIAN GUAY-POLIQUIN

TRANSLATED BY DAVID HOMEL

TALONBOOKS

Talonbooks
9259 Shaughnessy Street, Vancouver, British Columbia, Canada v6p 6r4
talonbooks.com

Talonbooks is located on xʷməθkʷəy̓əm, Sḵwx̱wú7mesh, and səl̓ilwətaʔɬ Lands.

First printing: 2019

Typeset in Sabon
Printed and bound in Canada on 100% post-consumer recycled paper

Interior design by Typesmith, cover design by Typesmith and andrea bennett

Talonbooks acknowledges the financial support of the Canada Council for the Arts, the Government of Canada through the Canada Book Fund, and the Province of British Columbia through the British Columbia Arts Council and the Book Publishing Tax Credit.

This work was originally published in French as *Le poids de la neige* by Éditions La Peuplade, Saguenay, Québec, in 2016. We acknowledge the financial support of the Government of Canada through the National Translation Program for Book Publishing, an initiative of the *Roadmap for Canada's Official Languages 2013–2018: Education, Immigration, Communities*, for our translation activities.

LIBRARY AND ARCHIVES CANADA CATALOGUING IN PUBLICATION

Guay-Poliquin, Christian, 1982–
[Poids de la neige. English]
 The weight of snow : a novel / Christian Guay-Poliquin; translated by David Homel.

Translation of: Le poids de la neige.
ISBN 978-1-77201-222-4 (SOFTCOVER)

 I. Homel, David, translator II. Title. III. Title: Poids de la neige. English

PS8613.U297P6513 2019   C843'.6   C2018-906167-7

For André B. Thomas

today
time turned the snow to metal
and the silence rejoiced

to form a perfect union
the white strokes rush groundward

mountains grab onto
the bark of trees and on
spiny arms

the greens disappear
the blues become opalescent
the edges of the browns and russets
fade

at times
a bird will draw a black line
across this accelerated space

—J.-N. POLIQUIN, winter 1984

I. LABYRINTH

Look. This place is vaster than any human life. Anyone who would try to flee will be forced to retrace his steps. Anyone who thinks he is moving in a straight line is describing great concentric circles. Here, everything slips away from your hands and your eyes. Here, forgetfulness of the world outside is stronger than any memory. Look again. This labyrinth offers no way out. Wherever our eyes fall, it is there. Look closer. No monster, no famished beast crouches in its corridors. But we are caught in the trap. Either we wait until the days and nights defeat us. Or we fashion ourselves wings and escape.

THIRTY-EIGHT

This is the land of snow, and it does not share its domain. It dominates the landscape, it weighs upon the mountains. The trees bow, they reach for the earth, their backs bent. Only the great spruce refuse to give in. They take their punishment, straight and black. They trace the end of the village and the beginning of the forest.

By my window, the birds come and go, quarrel, and scratch for food. From time to time, one of them will observe the quiet house with a worried eye.

On the frame outside, a thin branch stripped bare has been attached horizontally as a kind of barometer. If it points upward, the weather will be clear and dry. If it points down, there will be snow. Right now the weather is uncertain; the branch is in mid-journey of its trajectory.

It must be late. The grey sky is opaque and without nuance. The sun could be anywhere. A few snowflakes dance in the air and hang onto every second. A hundred steps from the house, in the clearing, Matthias is pushing a long stick into the snow. It looks like the mast of a ship, but without sails or flags.

Drops of water shiver on the roofline and slip down to the tips of the icicles. When the sun comes out, they sparkle like sharpened blades. From time to time, one of them will pull away, fall, and stab the snow. A dagger thrust into immensity.

But the snow is invincible. Soon it will reach the bottom of my window. Then the top. Then I will be blind.

This is winter. The days are short and frigid. The snow shows its teeth. The great expanse of space shrinks.

THIRTY-NINE

The window frame is damp. The wood stained by spongy, tinted circles. When it gets very cold, they are covered with crystals of frost. A little like lichen.

Logs crackle in the woodstove. From my bed, I can see the glittering coals through the air vent. The stove is ancient, a massive piece. Its doors creak when they open. This heap of black, burning cast iron is the centre of our lives.

I am alone on the porch. Everything is motionless. Everything in its place. The stool by the entrance, the rocking chair, the kitchen utensils, everything. A strange golden cylinder sits on the table. It was not there this morning. Matthias must have gone to the other side. But I noticed nothing.

Pain leaves me no respite. It holds me, it grips me, it possesses me. To tolerate it, I close my eyes and imagine I am at the wheel of my car. If I concentrate, I can hear the motor roaring. And see the landscapes go by, dazzled by the vanishing point of the road. But when I open my eyes, reality crushes me. I am bound to this bed, my legs imprisoned by two heavy splints. My car a heap of twisted metal somewhere beneath the snow. I am no longer the master of my fate.

My stomach breaks the silence. I am hungry. I feel weak and stiff. On the bedside table, some crumbs of black bread and the remains of oily coffee. Matthias will be back any time now.

FORTY-ONE

The door opens and a gust of cold air blows into the room. Matthias comes in and drops an armful of wood next to the stove. The logs crash to the floor and shards of bark go flying.

Matthias pulls off his coat, kneels down, and stirs the fire with a poker. Behind him, the snow from his boots begins melting and seeks its level on the uneven floor.

It's not very cold, he tells me, holding his hands toward the source of heat, but it's damp. It chills you to the bone.

When the flames begin to growl and lick the iron frame, Matthias closes the stove doors, puts the soup pot on to warm, and turns in my direction. His bushy eyebrows and white hair, and the deep wrinkles criss-crossing his forehead make him look like a mad scientist.

I have something for you.

I give him a questioning look. Matthias picks up the gold cylinder from the table and hands it to me. He gives me a big smile. The cylinder is heavy and telescopic. Its ends are covered in glass. I examine it from all angles. It is a spyglass. Like the ones sailors used long ago to pick out the thin line of the coast, or the enemy's ships.

Look outside.

I sit up in bed, extend the sliding tube, and place it against my eye. Everything moves toward me and each object takes on precise dimensions. As if I were on the other side of the window. The black flight of the birds, the footsteps in the snow, the unreal calm of the village, the edge of the forest.

Keep looking.

I know this landscape by heart. I have been watching it for some time now. I do not really remember the summer because of the fever and the drugs, but I did see the slow movement of the landscape, the grey autumn sky, the reddening light of the trees. I saw the ferns devoured by frost, the tall grass breaking when a breeze rose up, the first flakes landing upon the frozen ground. I saw the tracks of the animals that inspected the area after the first snow. The sky has swallowed everything up ever since. The landscape is in waiting. Everything has been put off until spring.

Nature with no respite. The mountains cut off the horizon, the forest hems us in on all sides, and the snow blinds us.

Look harder, Matthias tells me.

I examine the long stick that Matthias set up in the clearing. He has added minute graduation marks on it.

It's for measuring snow, he announces, triumphant.

With the spyglass, I can see the snow has reached forty-one centimetres. I consider the whiteness of the landscape a moment, then slump back on my bed and close my eyes.

Great, I tell myself. Now we can put numbers to our distress.

FORTY-TWO

Matthias is preparing black bread. A kind of brick made of buckwheat flower and molasses. According to him, it's filling and nutritious. And the best thing, since we have to ration our supplies as we wait for the next delivery.

Like an old shaman, he mixes, kneads, and shapes the dough with a striking economy of effort. When he finishes, he shakes off his clothes in a cloud of flour and cooks the cakes of black bread directly on the stovetop.

The weather has cleared. I observe the houses in the village, among the trees, at the foot of the hill. Most of them show no signs of life, though a few chimneys send up generous plumes of smoke. The grey columns rise straight into the sky as if refusing to melt into the vastness. There are twelve houses. Thirteen with ours. With the spyglass the village seems close by, but that is an illusion. I would need more than an hour to walk there. And I still can't get out of bed.

I believe the solstice has passed. The sun's path through the sky is still short, but the days have grown longer without us really noticing. New Year's Day must be behind us. Though I am not really sure. It makes no difference. I lost all notion of time long ago. Along with the desire to speak. No one can resist the silence, chained to broken legs, in the winter, in a village without electricity.

We still have a good supply of wood, but it is going down fast. We live in a porch made of drafts, and several times a night Matthias wakes up to feed the stove. When the wind blows, we can feel the cold holding us in the palm of its hand.

They will be sending us wood and supplies in a few days. In the meantime, I keep repeating that even if I survived a terrible car wreck, I still can't do anything for myself.

A crescent moon embraces the black sky. A thick, shiny crust has formed on the snow. In the glow of the night, it is like a calm, shimmering sea.

In the room, the oil lamp casts its light on the walls, sketching out golden shadows. Matthias comes to me with a bowl of soup and a piece of black bread. It is all we eat. The end of one soup is the beginning of the next. When we reach the bottom of the kettle, Matthias adds water and anything else he can get his hands on. When we have meat, he boils the bones and gristle to make broth. Vegetables, dry bread, it all ends up in the soup. Every day, at every meal, we eat that bottomless soup.

Matthias sits at the table, hands clasped carefully, in an attitude of contemplation, as I swallow down as much as I can. Often I finish my meal before he has started his.

At the beginning, Matthias had to force me to eat so I would recuperate and get my strength back. He would help me sit up and feed me patiently, one spoonful at a time, like a child. Now I can lean back on the pillows by myself. The pain and fatigue persist, but my appetite has returned. When he gets his hands on a few litres of milk, he makes cheese with the rennet he found in the creamery in the stable. Sometimes he gives cheese to the villagers, but often it is so good we devour all of it in a few days, right out of the cloth it has drained in.

Getting over my injuries takes a lot of energy. So does evaluating the passage of time. Maybe I should be like Matthias and just say *before the snow* or *since the snow*. But that would be too easy.

There has not been electricity for months. At the beginning, I was told, there were blackouts in the village. Nothing too worrisome. People practically got used to it. It would last a few hours, then the power would return. One morning, it did not come back. Not here, and not anywhere else. It was summer. People looked on the bright side. But when autumn came, they had to think about what to do next. As if they had been taken by surprise. It is winter now, and no one can do anything about it. In the houses, everyone gathers around the woodstove and a few blackened kettles.

Matthias finishes his bowl of soup and pushes it toward the centre of the table.

For a moment, nothing happens. I have a particular affection for these time outs that follow our meals.

They do not last long.

Matthias stands, picks up the dishes, and scours them in the sink. Then he wraps the pieces of bread in a plastic bag, folds the clothes that were drying on the line above the stove, extends the wick on the oil lamp, takes out the first aid kit, and brings over a chair.

Matthias clears his throat as if he was preparing to read aloud. But he says nothing, and turns his neck right and left to get rid of the tension. Then he pulls away the quilt that covers my legs.

I look away. Maybe Matthias thinks I am looking outside, but I can see his reflection perfectly in the dark window. One by one, he unties the straps from my right side. He slips his hand under my heel and raises my leg.

My heart beats faster. The pain roars and stares me down like a powerful, graceful beast.

Patiently, Matthias unwraps my bandages. He is slow and methodical. When he reaches the last layers of gauze, I feel the cloth sticking to my skin because of the humidity and the blood, and the infection too. He cuts off the rest of the bandage with scissors and pulls it away with calculated care. I breathe in deeply and concentrate on the air that fills my rib cage. Matthias moves his head back. I picture him evaluating the redness, the swelling, the bony callus, the shape of the tibia and the knee.

Pretty soon it will be time to take out the stitches, he says, disinfecting the wound.

The burning sensation is intense. I feel like my flesh is melting off my bones.

Don't move! Matthias thunders. Let me do my work.

I try to look away as far as possible from my legs, toward

the back of the room and the two doors. The front door and the one that leads the other way. I look at the heavy, squatting woodstove, the objects on the shelves, the ceiling with its beams squared off with an axe. Two light bulbs hang there like dinosaur skeletons in a museum.

Matthias takes a tube out of the first aid kit and tries to decipher the label. With a sigh, he slips his glasses from his shirt pocket and sets them on the end of his nose.

This should do.

Before rewrapping my bandages, he applies a thick layer of ointment to my wound. It is cold, and offers some relief for a few seconds. Until he tightens the straps around the splint that keeps my leg in place and my pulse starts beating at my temples. I grab at the sheets and curse my fate. Matthias starts talking. His lips move, but I hear nothing. I think he is trying to tell me that it's over now. After a few seconds the pain subsides a little and then, as if we were at a great distance from each other, his voice reaches me, barely audible.

Just take it, he says, take it, we have to do the other leg now.

I think it snowed a little during the night, but this morning the sky is blue and hard. The icicles glitter from the roofline.

On the stove, a kettle filled with snow. Back in the fall, Matthias would draw water directly from the stream that flows down toward the village. It was clear and transparent, and tasted of smooth stones and roots. Some mornings, he had to break through the ice to fill his bucket. At first all he had to do was lean on the surface, but soon he had to use a branch, then a hatchet. One day he got tired of it and started melting snow. It does not taste the same, but I can't complain. Matthias does everything here. He feeds the stove, cooks, and empties the pot I use as a toilet. He is the one who decides, disposes, takes responsibility. He is the master of time and space.

And I am powerless. I do not have the strength, and even less so the mobility. I don't have the energy to communicate, interact, converse. Nor the desire. I prefer to ruminate on my misfortune in silence. At the beginning Matthias did not understand why I kept quiet. With time I think he has gotten used to it.

Since my accident, I have had trouble retracing the chain of events. With the pain, fever, and fatigue, the usual duration of days and weeks has been disrupted by the impatience of snow. Everything happened so fast. The accident, the watchmen, the operation, then I found myself here, with Matthias. I know very well he wanted nothing to do with me. My presence makes him ill at ease and bothers him. His plans have been upset. Since the power went out, nothing has happened the way he anticipated.

When they found me underneath my car, the watchmen saw I was finished. There was nothing anyone could do. My legs had been crushed by the impact. I had lost a lot of blood. By a stroke of luck, when they shined their light, someone thought he recognized me. And he convinced the others to bring me to the village.

It was raining. Torrents of water streamed down over the forest. I remember that much, the people carrying me had trouble making progress in the mud. There was no doctor in the village. Only a veterinarian and a pharmacist. Since the power went out, they were taking care of the injured and sick. They took care of the worst cases too, when there was no more cause for hope.

I was lying in a bed in a narrow, dim room. They had wrapped my legs in thick bandages and handcuffed my wrists to the bed-frame. Some light managed to slip between the planks of the boarded-up window. Every time I lifted my head to see where I was, a lightning bolt of pain shot through my body.

People were coming to my bedside all the time. To bring me food. Give me pills. Ask me questions. My name? Where was I heading? What happened with the accident? I was in enormous pain, and the world was reduced to a few shapes bending over me as they might bend over a bottomless well. They insisted I answer the questions they asked over and over again. I could scream and struggle all I wanted, no one seemed to understand what I was trying to say. They must have wondered if they should cut short my suffering or make the effort to take care of me.

When they finally left me alone, I tried to listen to what was going on in the room next door. People were coming and going. Sometimes they raised their voices and I managed to decipher the conversation. Other times they whispered and nothing was audible.

The accident was violent. I was in a state of confusion. I dreamed of my car. I searched for my father. My memories overlapped. I pictured the scene over and over again. Days and nights on the road. The black-out, the gas stations pillaged, the militia by the side of the roads, panic in the cities. And suddenly, a few kilometres from the village, in the tired glow of my headlights, two arms lifted skyward. Tires squealing on the pavement. The attempt at evasive action. The heavy impact. The blood. The cracks in the windshield. The car rolling over. My body thrown from it. Then the weight of the metal on my legs.

I had left the village more than ten years earlier. Ten years and no word from me, or almost none. I buried the past and thought I would never come back. But the watchman had no doubt who I was and he insisted I be taken care of. His voice was clear from the other side of the wall.

Enough is enough. We can't leave him to die like that. Don't you recognize him? He's the mechanic's son. He left here a long time ago. He's in a state of shock, but give him a chance. His father just died, but he still has family in the village. His aunts and uncles live on the road that goes to the mine. I'll go fetch them.

My aunts and uncles came. At first I thought I was seeing ghosts, then I heard their voices and tears came to my eyes.

Yes, my uncles confirmed, struck by the terrible shape I was in, that's him. My aunts held my hands and tried to comprehend what had happened to me. I was so happy to see them I couldn't say a single word.

The handcuffs, take off his handcuffs, my aunts demanded. Right now.

The people told them I had been agitated since I found out my father had died, and they had to be careful so I would not aggravate my injuries. My aunts and uncles went into the room next door. I knew they were discussing my situation, but I couldn't hear what they were saying. It sounded serious.

A little later, the veterinarian and the pharmacist came into the room. They sat down next to the bed. The veterinarian lit her headlamp and cut off the bandages that girded my legs. I watched her from the corner of my eye. Her face was familiar. Her features hardened when she saw how bad my injuries were. She turned to the pharmacist. He nodded his head. As she was putting on her mask and gloves, the veterinarian looked at me and I knew she had recognized me too. The pharmacist put a sponge over my mouth and nose, and she told me to count to ten. Her voice. Yes, her voice reminded me of something. Her voice echoed back to me, but I could not remember her name. The beam of her lamp swept the room. Then everything went black.

When I came to, I had no idea where I was. Luckily my aunts were at my bedside. I heard them discussing in low voices. I lifted my head and saw that my legs were tightly held in solid wooden splints. When my aunts realized I was awake, they rushed to comfort me.

Don't worry. The operation was a success. You'll be fine. You'll make it out of here. Here, drink some water. You need to rest. You have to get your strength back. Yes, rest up.

A few moments later, I was exhausted. I lapsed back into nightmares of chase, a famished beast, a labyrinth. They pursued one another in a single incoherent dream.

The next day or the day after, I'm not sure, the watchman returned to see me. Finally he took off my handcuffs. He brought me water, a piece of bread, and a can of tuna. He used the opportunity to ask questions, too. When he saw I was not answering, he kept quiet for a while, then changed his strategy.

Even if the electricity ends up coming back, things won't be the same. You know, everything that happened since the blackout has disfigured our lives. Here we're probably getting along better than in the city, but it's still not easy. At first people stuck together, then some of them panicked, a few left the village, and others tried to take advantage of the situation. Since then calm has been restored. We distribute food and make our rounds and keep an eye on things. But we have to be vigilant. Everything could go wrong at any time.

The veterinarian and the pharmacist arrived and interrupted the watchman.

How is he doing?

Not too bad.

The veterinarian examined my legs while the pharmacist had me swallow a handful of pills.

He doesn't have a fever, the veterinarian said after she took my temperature.

That's because of what I'm giving him, the pharmacist told her. That, and only that.

The veterinarian came to me and said my legs were fractured in several places. She had operated in a similar way in the past several times, but only on cows, horses, and dogs.

I looked at her and smiled.

She ran her hand through my hair.

You'll make it all right.

Then the two of them, along with the watchman, went into the room next door. I heard the pharmacist's voice through the wall.

He survived the accident and reacted well to the operation, but sooner or later his wounds are going to get infected. It's inevitable. He will need a lot of antibiotics and analgesics, and our stocks are limited.

They wondered who was going to take care of me. My aunts and uncles, no doubt. With the blackout, everyone was overworked. There was too much to do. Who else would have time to look after a gravely injured man? Care for him, feed him, wash him?

Then their voices dropped and I lost the thread of the conversation.

A few days later, my legs were swollen and my wounds were so painful I could hardly breathe. I was shivering and sweating. I needed help for everything. People came and went by my bedside. They covered their ears to keep from hearing my feverish lamentations.

Twice a day, Maria came and gave me a shot. That allowed me a few hours' respite before the pain returned to blur my vision.

I knew it, the pharmacist sighed. I knew we would end up giving him all the medication we have.

With the pills and shots, I managed to sleep a little. But when I opened my eyes, I had no idea whether I had slept a few minutes, a few hours, or a few days. Often I dreamed I was pinned to the ground and that someone was cutting off my legs with an axe. It wasn't a nightmare. I felt a sudden liberation.

My aunts and uncles came to visit me frequently. Even if everything around me was a theatre of shadows, I could hear them talking, telling stories, making jokes. Then, one day, they explained they couldn't wait anymore. It was hunting season. A number of families had already taken to the woods. The electricity was not coming back and food had to be put up before winter.

We're going to the hunting camp, they announced. We'll be back in a few weeks with meat, a lot of meat. We wish you could come with us, but that wouldn't work. In the meantime, don't worry, you're in good hands. We were promised they would take good care of you. You have to do your part and work on getting better.

They each said their goodbyes, then they left. I wished I could have made them stay.

Some time later a group came into my room. The watchman, the veterinarian, and the pharmacist were there. Someone began speaking, telling me it was out of the question for me to stay here, in this house. I felt their eyes running along the walls, slipping to the floor, and disappearing into the cracks between the planks. No one wanted the extra burden. Maybe they should have left me to my fate under the car. Then the veterinarian broke the silence and offered to take care of me until my family returned. The pharmacist cut her off immediately.

That makes no sense, we can't have him in our house. We did what we could. We have other patients to look after.

The watchman stepped forward as if he wanted to make a suggestion. But he kept his mouth shut.

I can solve the problem, the pharmacist went on, in a way that will ease the burden on everyone. You can see how much pain he's in.

The veterinarian stared at the watchman, who was standing in the middle of the room. And that's when, if I remember rightly, he mentioned the old man who had come to live in the house at the top of the hill.

You know, the old guy who showed up at the beginning of the summer. He had car trouble, he was looking for a mechanic. Then the power went off and he couldn't leave. He started living in the house on the hill. Sometimes we see him when he comes down to the village. He's always saying he needs to get back to the city, and that the woman next door to where he lived is going to come for him one of these days. But she never showed up. Nobody believes his story, but everyone knows he always accepts the rations we give him. I came across him the other day near the church. We talked. He's old, that's for sure. But he looks in good shape. And he's a lot more lucid than people like to think.

Him? the pharmacist said, surprised. He tried to steal a pickup truck a while back. I caught him just as he was breaking into it. He pretended nothing was up, as usual. He's a wily old bastard. But why not? We could fob off our injury case on him.

FORTY-FIVE

In the morning, every morning, Matthias does his exercises. With the concentration of an alchemist, he carries out a series of odd postures, lengthy stretches, and quick contractions. Sometimes he maintains the same position for several minutes. His immobility is powerful and subterranean. Generally he accompanies his movements with deep breathing. He bends, straightens, contorts. His gestures are broad and flexible. When he breathes out, you can hear the strength of his diaphragm, as if he is fighting, with great slowness, a stranger, a bear, or a monster. Then, without warning, he stops completely and stands straight with an air of triumph. His day can begin.

The sky lightened some time ago, but the sun has scarcely made it above the forest. At certain spots its rays have pierced the trellis of trees. I take out my spyglass and examine the surroundings. The snow is unmarked except for Matthias's heavy footprints and the skittish traces of squirrels. The other animals have retreated deeper into the woods. They can concentrate on surviving that way, far from our eyes.

Matthias is making coffee. Since there is not much of it, he mixes two spoonfuls of grounds with one of fresh coffee.

That was exactly what he was doing when I was brought here. Strange how clear my memory is of the smell in the room. Matthias opened the door to the veterinarian who was standing before him in the rain. Behind her, the watchman and the pharmacist were carrying me on a stretcher. Matthias invited everyone in for coffee.

Fever and antibiotics had cast me into a state of lethargy that had nothing to do with sleep. I was in a sort of passive wakefulness, halfway between a coma and a coherent dream. I did not move, I did not speak, but I heard everything.

Who is he? Matthias asked as he bent over me.

The mechanic's son, the veterinarian told him. He was in a car accident.

The watchman looked around the room. There was a wood-stove, a rocking chair, a table, and a sofa. A single bed bordered the window.

You're well set up here, he remarked.

The house was abandoned. I fixed up this room in the meantime.

In the meantime?

Matthias hesitated.

Until the neighbour lady comes, he said finally. She's taking her time, but she's going to come for me. For sure. She knows I have to get back to town. She understands.

The watchman rubbed his chin.

You've been saying that for a while now. Why do you want to go back to the city so much? It's eight hours by car in good conditions, and you know, with the power out, you can't get around like you used to. There are roadblocks everywhere, militias, highwaymen. They say it's chaos in the city, accidents at every corner, the stores looted, people fleeing. Maybe your neighbour had a problem, the watchman said, weighing his words.

She'll come, Matthias insisted. She'll come.

What if she doesn't? What are you going to do? Steal a truck?

Matthias kept his eyes fastened on the grounds in his coffee cup.

There's no more gas anywhere, you know.

I have to get back to town, Matthias repeated.

They stood there in silence, as if the discussion had come to an end. Then the watchman started talking again.

We're lucky here, our village is hidden in the middle of the forest. Having no power complicates things, but at least everything is under control. We watch the entrance to the village, we consolidate our resources, we help each other out.

Matthias did not react. He waited for what would come next.

You know some people are talking about making an expedition if the outage continues. The idea is to get in contact with the outside world. They would go to the villages along the coast, then to the city. Some of them want to find family members who live there. That's normal, you know, when you haven't had news from relatives in a long time.

The watchman paused for effect and cast a glance in my direction. At the time, I remember, with the fog of medication, I had to concentrate to follow what was happening around me.

I have a proposal for you, the watchman went on. You look after him and we'll keep a spot for you in the convoy that will be going to the city. From now on, you'll get two shares of rations. That way you'll manage. And you won't have to go down to the village, I'll come by and bring it to you.

Matthias looked out the window.

I have to get back to town before winter.

I understand, the watchman went on, but it takes time to organize an expedition. You have to find gas, food, equipment. You have to consider security, and plan out the itinerary. No one wants to get caught by winter, you know, especially when there are no more plows clearing the roads.

When will you be leaving?

Spring.

This spring? Matthias said, discouraged.

Yes, this spring. As soon as the roads are passable.

That's too late, Matthias complained, how am I going to get along?

You're going to be patient and you're going to take care of him. That will be your contribution. Then you'll have your spot in the convoy.

He's in bad shape, Matthias muttered, looking at my splints.

Yes, but he'll make it.

You think so? Matthias questioned, raising his eyebrows.

The veterinarian wanted to step in, but the pharmacist motioned her to wait. Matthias paced the room.

What about wood for the stove?

I'll see to it, the watchman promised, I'll bring everything you need.

Matthias thought it over.

I'll stop by once a week, the veterinarian said, to give you a hand and see how he's progressing.

Matthias nodded.

Put him over there, he said reluctantly, pointing to the bed by the window. I'll sleep on the sofa.

The watchman and the pharmacist did as he asked.

Come here, the veterinarian suggested. I'm going to change his bandages with you, that way you'll know how to do it.

The pharmacist took out a roll of gauze, the first aid kit, and the jars of pills. The watchman sat on the stool by the door
and lit a cigarette.

Doesn't he talk? Matthias asked.

Not really, the watchman answered, you know, with the accident and the medication, that's normal. And I suppose his father dying shook him up pretty bad. At least I think so. Give him time.

Once the veterinarian saw that Matthias had understood her instructions, they tightened my splints and threw the soiled bandages into the burning stove.

If you run out of ointment, she added, you can put sugar on his wounds. That will fight the infection. But remember to always give him his antibiotics.

There are pills for pain, the pharmacist pointed out. That should quiet him down if he complains too much.

The watchman thanked Matthias, then motioned to his comrades to leave. As he was crossing the threshold after them, Matthias put his hand on his shoulder.

What if he doesn't make it?

Come and get us as quickly as you can. But remember, his life is in your hands.

I'll do what I can, Matthias stammered, taken aback.

Everything will be fine, the watchman assured him as he went out the door. I'll be back in a few days with the wood and supplies.

What's your name? Matthias asked. You didn't tell me your name.

Joseph. She's Maria and her husband is José, he said, pointing to the veterinarian and the pharmacist.

Joseph left, and Matthias stood in the doorway for a long time.

Maria, that's it, her name is Maria, I thought. Then the fog overtook me again.

I am alone in the room. Matthias went out on his snowshoes. I pull on the old quilt that covers my feet. At the end of the bed, kilometres away, my toes are the colour of bruises, but at least they move. With the splints, they are the only part that is mobile.

Pain is still my master, but at least the bouts of fever have subsided. I have stopped waking up suddenly, gasping for breath, trying to figure out where I am. I have learned to recognize the room, the window next to my bed, and Matthias's face. When I open my eyes, I know where I am, who I am, and what awaits me.

Not long after I was delivered here, my temperature shot up and my teeth started chattering. Matthias sat at my bedside. He put on fresh bandages and changed the sheets that were soaked in sweat. He wiped my face, my neck, and applied cold compresses to my body. He spoke to me too. I don't know what he said, he told me all kinds of things, stories, adventures, it was like the odyssey of a man pursued by a furious god, and all he wants is to get back home after twenty years of absence. In the morning, he broke off his story and went for a nap on the couch. When he woke up later, he lifted my head, gave me something to drink and some pills. They were all the colours of the rainbow. During the day, I struggled against an invisible abyss. At night I slept with my eyes open. The way the dead do.

Often I dreamed I was running. I was running full out through the corridors of a labyrinth. Everywhere I went a red thread lay on the ground. I ran as if a beast were on my trail. I didn't see it, but it was there, behind me. I clearly heard its panting breath and the clatter of its hooves. It was closing in. Its claws cut through the air, trying to tear off my legs. I kept on running. I was dreaming and I didn't look back.

At the worst of the fever I must have lost consciousness, because I remember waking up, gasping for air, in Matthias's arms. We were outside, in the pouring rain. My body was on fire and the ice-cold water helped bring me back to this world. When I regained consciousness, Matthias lifted his head to the sky as if he too had been saved. The rain poured down his face and his hair was plastered to his forehead. Then he picked me up and carried me inside. It wasn't easy. We were soaked and I had trouble clinging to his neck. When he laid me on the bed, I was so weak I felt I was sinking into the blankets. Matthias fell to his knees and tried to catch his breath.

Over the days that followed, my fever broke and I stabilized. At the time I felt nothing outside of a tingling sensation. Then a sharp, cutting pain took hold of my body. As if thousands of nails were piercing my flesh from the inside, slashing though my spine, driving into the palms of my hands, my feet, fastening me to the bed. A black frozen pain opened my eyes in the depths of the night and made me fear I would never walk again.

The analgesics Matthias had me take reduced the agony, but they lasted only a few hours. Sometimes he would massage my legs. He would sit on my bed, take off the heavy gauze, clean my wounds, and rub my thighs, calves, and feet. I did not like him kneading me like black bread. But he was careful when it came to my wounds. After every session, the swelling subsided and I didn't feel so cold.

My toes are still moving at the far end of my body. I believe my bones are knitting together, my wounds are closing, and the penicillin is doing its job. But the pain is tenacious, constant, tireless. I pull away the cover to look at my legs. My splints are recycled wooden slats, and belts were nailed to them instead of the usual straps. On one of the slats, I can see saw-tooth marks. On the other the trace of a hinge pulled off with a claw hammer. I am a monster fashioned from cast-off wood, bolts, and pieced-together flesh. But that's better than nothing.

The hospitals are far away. In space and in time.

FORTY-SEVEN

It is the end of the afternoon. When he came back from his walk, Matthias stoked the fire, then went looking for a book on the other side. He reads a lot, and since I show no interest in the books he leaves by my bed, he tells me stories. Like the one about the two tramps quarrelling beneath a tree as they wait for someone who never shows up.

Every time he crosses over to the other side, a cold draft rushes through the half-open door. And every time, the draft rouses me from my lethargy and I lift my head to look into the great lifeless house. But I can see no more than a dark hallway with a light at the end.

We live in the annex of a great manor, in the summer kitchen. A porch with a wood stove and a wide window facing south. When the sky is clear, the light enters and warms the room. But as soon as the sun falls behind the horizon, we have to stoke the fire. Though it shows signs of wear and a few stains caused by leaks, the room seems to have been designed with care. The moldings feature rosette figures. The floors are hardwood. On the walls, you can pick out spots where pictures once hung.

In the centre of the porch floor is a trap door. It gives onto a crawl space. Matthias uses it as a cellar. He stores meat there, and vegetables, and everything that needs to be kept cool but not freeze.

The ceiling is criss-crossed by broad wooden beams that follow the gentle incline. In the summer, I imagine the rain must drum upon the sheet-metal roof. A sort of roll that would recall the comforting interior of cars and the weightlessness of long trips. But for now the snow piles up without a sound. When I listen hard, I hear nothing more than the beams sighing above our heads.

Matthias stands in the doorway. He looks like a navigator in the prow of a ship.

Guess what I found, he says, eager for my answer.

For a moment, the door gapes open behind him. The corridor disappears into the shadows and appears to open into a spacious salon. I picture a manor with high ceilings, comfortable rooms, and hallways branching off. A labyrinth of sorts: some rooms lead into others, but some are dead ends. A wide staircase leads upstairs, there must be a chandelier above the dining room table, an imposing library, and a stone fireplace in the sitting room. One thing is for sure, the house is too big for us. It would be impossible to heat, we would burn up our wood supply in the space of few weeks. Then we would die of cold after burning the furniture.

You give up? Matthias asks.

He stares, waiting for an answer that never comes.

It's a chess set, he says, sighing. I thought you might enjoy it.

He closes the door with his hip. The labyrinth on the other side disappears as quickly as it appeared and the walls of the porch close in on us.

The wind rose in the night. Squalls shook the porch. It has begun to snow. I hear it beating against the window like birds deceived by their reflections.

From this side of the dark glass, I observe my face. A large, dark stain of shadow, haggard eyes, greasy hair, unkempt beard. Under the covers, the flat outline of my prone body, thin, useless.

Matthias is in the rocking chair. He is repairing one of the straps on his snowshoes. The oil lamp shivers. Soot is slowly smearing the glass bell. The wick should be trimmed, but Matthias does not react, too absorbed by the task at hand.

We have finished eating. The dishes washed, the floor swept, the wood stacked. Everything as it should be. I don't know how he does it. The hours run together, the days repeat, and Matthias gets busy. He never stops, except to read. From dawn to dusk, he toils, cleans, cooks. He works slowly, never hurried. The way the snow falls. And he is right. He has to do something. Winter roars, the blackout takes us further back in time, and losing touch is the most pressing danger.

Even if I won't accept my fate, I have to accept that I am lucky to have ended up here. Maybe I will never walk again, I have lost all desire to speak, but I'm not dead. At least, not yet.

As he sews the leather strap, Matthias watches me from the corner of his eye.

You know, during the world wars, some conscripts refused to join the army, he begins. Some of them got married in a hurry, and others, like my father, went and hid in the woods and hoped they'd be forgotten. But taking to the forest wasn't easy. The winters were harder back then. And bounty-hunters had all the patience they needed to watch the outskirts of the village for the slightest sign of life. A rifle shot, a plume of smoke, an unusual path in the snow. Military justice was generous when it came to denunciations or information that would let them locate and hunt down deserters. But most of the time, the villages supported them secretly. Provisions were left at strategic points. The poor guys came to get the stuff in the middle of the night, attracting no attention, and returned to the mountains to pursue their desperate survival. Even in the depth of winter, they lit a fire only once darkness had fallen, and when the nights were clear, it was wiser not to stir the embers from the previous day. Deep in their hiding places, the young men busied themselves the best they could as they stared at the forest moving in on them. They darned their clothes, played cards, and polished their hunting rifles. Sometimes tensions grew, and when they switched sentinel duty, they would cast wary glances at their fellows. Yet they knew they could not do without each other. If they wanted to survive, they would have to face the cold, hunger, and boredom together. They soon understood that the most important job was, without a doubt, to tell stories to each other.

The wind is still blowing. The squalls pummel Matthias's story and make the walls of the porch groan.

Resisters and deserters, it comes down to the same thing, Matthias went on. All of them had to spend the winter in some shelter, hunkered down in the middle of nowhere, saving their energy as they waited for spring. Spring, with its liberation. With a guy like you, he tells me, it wouldn't have worked. We would have been discovered or would have killed each other. No one can survive with someone who won't talk.

I awake. The sun is high in the sky and the blanket of snow lustrous with cold. Blinding. I slept poorly last night, my legs hurt, pain seized my bones. I could not close my eyes.

Kneeling in front of the plastic basin, Matthias is doing the washing. He rubs our clothes hard with detergent and hangs them on the line above the stove.

He gets on my nerves. Not only is he indefatigable, he is surprisingly agile. He leans over, straightens, and pivots as if his age were a simple disguise. When he drops something, he often catches it before it hits the floor. He is flexible and energetic. Slow at times, but always flexible and energetic.

Often he works without a word, though sometimes he talks too much. When he changes my bandages, when he stokes the fire, when he stirs the soup, when he washes the dishes, he chatters, he chats, he recites. I never answer. After all, he is only thinking out loud.

He was brought up in a world buried under work and days, he often says. Just before the great wars. The streets of his village were unpaved. The houses were bursting with children who wore hand-me-down boots with holes. Life in its entirety revolved around hard work and a few prayers.

Those were different days, he goes on, I would slip away from the family uproar and go to watch the blacksmith across the way hammer the metal and talk to the horses. If I really concentrate, I can still hear his raspy voice and smell the scent of burnt hoof, the fire, the iron. That was the only place where I could believe in something else. As if every animal newly shod could carry me somewhere far away. My parents died young and with them died their way of being, I took over the house and little by little the past fell silent. The flame had gone out in the heart of the forge. The newspapers shouted news of the future and fresh promises hurried to seduce us. A few kilometres distant, we could see the bony structure of the city rising. Dreams came from all directions in scrolls of smoke, there was talk of lighting the streets, digging tunnels, sending up buildings higher than steeples. My children were born, the fields fell prey to pavement, the church disappeared behind office towers. The family dwelling was lost in the corridors of intersections, fast lanes, and billboards. Everywhere you looked, cranes were harassing the horizon, a thick odour of asphalt weighed upon the roofs, in the streets the belly of the city was being opened up and sewn back again. From my balcony I heard the song of sirens. Sometimes I saw flashing lights speed by, other times not. The misfortunes were distant and anonymous. Then the children left and the house became very big and very empty. The rooms echoed with the ticking of clocks. My wife and I were alone to contemplate the endless construction sites, the sweaty foreheads of the workers, the rattling of steam shovels that lifted their arms like docile, powerful beasts. I remember the dust that floated in the beams of sunlight. When the grandchildren came to the house it was a blessing. My wife glowed with happiness. Even after fifty years of life together, I never grew tired of her beauty, her charm, her grace. But time is a thief. My wife started clinging ever tighter to the things she knew. Her memory wavered and her voice trailed off in the labyrinth of her words. She maintained an irritated, confused silence. Her movements became abrupt. Hesitation filled her eyes. I didn't know who, of the two of us, truly recognized the other. Then one day she fell in the bathroom. I felt the end was near. The phone, waiting for the ambulance. They took her a few blocks away, to a building of elevators and corridors. I visited her every day. Her eyes soon lost their colour, and nothing seemed to bother her anymore. She started smiling again, and showed no intention of returning from her enchanted island. She knew I would be there every day, by her side. With age and fatigue, the chronology of life blurred. We distrust our memories more than we do our forgetfulness. I needed time off. I needed fresh air. I left for a week in my old car. Drive, see the landscape. See the landscape, and drive. Take a long trip, then return and see my wife, my head clear. A few days later, my car broke down in the middle of the forest. I walked to the village in search of a mechanic. Then the electricity went off. At first I thought the neighbour lady would come and get me. That was what she said when I talked to her on the phone. All right, I'll get on the road tonight, I'll be there tomorrow. A few days later, she still had not shown up. The phone lines stopped working. I kept waiting. I didn't understand, she had always been a trustworthy person. I was desperate, I tried to steal a pickup truck, but didn't know how to go about it. In any case, all the gas had been siphoned off and people kept a jealous watch over their supplies. There was no way out. I decided to settle in here. Then one night the trap snapped shut. They brought me a feverish, crippled young man. That man was you.

Matthias is still bent over the basin, surrounded by a heap of clothes and a bucket of water. On the line above his head, the pants, shirts, socks, and underwear look like carefully sorted rags.

My wife is waiting for me, he explains, and he stops scrubbing. She is waiting for my visit. She waits every day. I promised her. I have to get back to town. I have to get back to her side. I have no choice. I promised. I promised never to abandon her. I promised to die with her.

Matthias's voice wavers. He will burst into tears at any moment.

Look, he says, pulling a photo from his pocket, that's her.

I don't know how to react. I pick up my spyglass and scan the empty landscape. The snow gauge shows the same amount as yesterday.

FIFTY-SIX

Today the sky has clouded over and the trees huddle together. The barometer is pointing downward. Maybe a storm on its way. It's hard to say. When the sky darkens we always imagine a storm is brewing. The chickadees chirp among the branches. When a blue jay makes an appearance, they scatter. As soon as it leaves, they return, one by one.

Matthias brings me a bowl of soup, a slab of black bread, and a few pills. He sits down at the table, absorbed in his meditations, as I take my first mouthful. After every meal, he takes stock of our supplies and stands in front of the trap door for several minutes. Then he sits me on the sofa to change my sheets. He takes me by the armpits to move me. As he holds me in his arms, my legs swing one way, then the other, as if I were a marionette.

From the sofa, I watch Matthias's silhouette against the brightness of the window. When he raises his arms, the sheets fill with air and settle gently on the bed. Like a spare parachute. I hear him ruminating, muttering, complaining. He may be talking to me, but his words seem stuck between his teeth. Strangely, as my eyelids grow heavy with the medication, his voice becomes clearer. As if he were speaking to me in my sleep, his words mixing in with my dreams. As if he were trying to penetrate my mind and cast a spell on me.

Before the snow started, you didn't want to eat anything and now you eat like a pig. Eating me out of house and home. I was afraid you'd die of your fever. But you got away every time. You're my obstacle, the stone in my path. And my ticket out of here. You can act like you're made of ice, I know you hang onto every word I speak. You can face pain, all right, but you're afraid of what comes next. That's why I tell you stories. Any kind of story. A shred of memory, ghosts, lies. Every time your face lights up. Not much, but enough. In the evening I tell you what I've read. I tell you everything sometimes, until dawn wipes away the night. Like the book I just finished, where all the stories flow together and run into the other a thousand and one times from one night to the next. I come from another world, another time, and you know it, it's obvious. More than a generation separates us, and everything points to the fact that you're the stubborn, grumbling old man. We are both living in the ruins, but words don't paralyze me the way they do you. That's my survival work, my mechanics, my luminous despair. Are you trying to measure up to me, maybe? Maybe you want a race between two human wrecks? You're not up to it. Just keep quiet. Keep your mouth shut tighter if you can, it's all the same to me. You are at my mercy. I could play your game, I could stop talking, you'd sink into the folds of your blankets. You want time to pass, but time frightens you. You want to take care of yourself by yourself, but you're not up to it. You're stuck here. You wander through the depths. Even the simplest movement is impossible for you. You spit on your fate. You can't get used to the fact that in the prime of life your body is broken and ground to dust. You're wary, I know, but you have learned to accept the care I give you. You're jealous of me too. Because I'm standing pat. Go ahead and look, and listen, I'm standing on my own two feet. Look, I'm twice your age and I'm standing tall.

Matthias stops. I hear him turn and move in my direction.

Since the snow started, the bouts of fever make you moan, and murmur, they drag a few words out of you. It's not conversation, but I settle for what you give me. At my age, when people cheat, it doesn't bother me anymore. Imagination is a form of courage. Look, look harder, look better, it's snowing and we don't even notice it, and time is going by. Soon, I say soon so as not to say later, much later, you'll be able to stand up, you'll hang onto me as you put one foot in front of the other and you'll go from the bed to the sofa by yourself. From the sofa to the chair. Then from the chair to the edge of the stove. You'll stare at the door every day a little harder. You'll weigh your words and not speak them. You'll calculate the depth of winter and curse the wonderland of storms. You'll probe the state of your injuries, the depth of our solitude, the laziness of spring, and our food supplies. You'll listen to me talk and I won't realize it, and you won't understand how you cheated death. Soon, I say soon so as not to say now, soon I won't have the strength to fight for the two of us. I won't be able to hide behind the slowness of my body or the few hopes I have cobbled together. But I will pretend. And I'll go on believing in your recovery, the days growing longer and the snow melting. Over and over I will bring back the sparks from the blacksmith's forge and the city spreading out and my wife's laughter. I'll tell you all kinds of things, I'll make it up if I have to. We've got no choice, it's the only way to confront what is coming. Don't worry. I'll be there, I'll look after everything. It will be all right. Don't worry, I'll pretend. There are only so many ways of surviving.

II. MAZE

Either we wait until the days and nights defeat
us. Or we fashion wings for ourselves and escape
through the air. We just need to stick some feathers on our arms with wax. Take flight, get air
beneath our wings. Afterward, nothing will
hold us back. But before we depart, listen to me
carefully. If you fly too low, the humidity will
weigh down your plumage and you'll crash to
the ground. If you fly too high, the sun's heat
will melt your wings and you'll plummet into
nothingness.

SIXTY-TWO

Yesterday, the wind turned calm and fat heavy flakes began to
fall. The snow continues to fall in tight ranks, in parallel formation. We can hardly make out the snow gauge. The trail that
Matthias left over the past days has been completely swallowed
up. A cottony silence has settled over everything. All I hear
are the flames licking the sides of the woodstove and Matthias
rolling out pie dough on the counter.

There is a knock on the door.

Matthias turns around, shakes the flour off his clothes, and
rushes to open the door. A man walks into the room, covered
with melting snow. He is carrying a bag on his back, and he sets
it down and goes to sit on the stool by the entrance. He pulls
off his coat and catches his breath. We quickly recognize the
man, his face, his beard, his high forehead. It's Joseph.

Matthias is happy to see him, and it shows. He offers to
make him coffee, then tells him to get warm by the stove.
Joseph thanks him, rolls up the sleeves of his woollen sweater,
and takes out his tobacco. Joseph lights his cigarette, sending
thick scrolls of smoke into the air. He gives us both a long look.
Matthias puts water on to boil and casts an eye at the bag our
visitor has brought, while I sit up as straight as I can in my bed.

And so, he asks, trying to hide a look of disapproval, how
are things?

At his feet, the snow is melting, turning to water, and forming a pool. It is as if he were sitting on a rock, looking off into the distance, toward our desert island.

SIXTY-THREE

In the village, Joseph begins, some people claim it's going to snow for the next few days. I don't know how they can read the clouds, but that's what they're saying. And they're saying· it's going to be a long winter. But you don't need a crystal ball to come to that conclusion. In any case, this is a lot of snow for this time of year. Even with my snowshoes, it's not easy to get up here. I think your house is moving a little further from the village every day.

When he speaks, Joseph waves his arms in the air and the ash falls off his cigarette, though he doesn't notice.

This week, a group of hunters came out of the woods. Everyone had given up hope of seeing them again. The rest of them had returned from their camps a long time ago. They wanted to avoid needless manoeuvres, so they waited until the ice on the lakes was thick enough to bear their weight. With all the moose carcasses they were bringing back, I can understand. In the village, everyone's busy salting the meat and putting it up. There's no prettier sight.

He stubbed out his cigarette and leaned over me.

But we still have no news of your family. In the village, some people are saying that they had trouble in the woods and got trapped in the snow. Who knows? People tell all kinds of stories. Maybe they decided to spend the winter in the woods, far from the blackout and everyone else. I'm not worried about them, they've seen it all before.

As Matthias serves us coffee, I picture my uncles and their hunting camp. It stands on the bank of a river, between two chains of mountains. At that spot, I remember, the water is fast and the riverbed is deep and green. To get across you need a canoe. On the other side, the cedars are enormous and moss carpets the ground. The camp is back from the river. You follow a path made of roots to reach it. When you spot the chimney through the trees, you're there. It's not very big, but there's room for everyone. They could very well spend the winter there.

You know, Joseph continues, we've had a few meetings in the village. Even with the blackout, Jude wanted to go on being mayor. At first we weren't too sure, but José threw his support behind him and everyone got used to the idea. After all, we're not so bad off, and we owe that to Jude. He does the coordination work, takes good care of our precious supply of gas, and distributes the provisions that were stored in the grocery. Since the blackout hit, half the population has deserted the village. People went to other villages, or the city, or maybe into the woods, who can say? Jude is right. No sense leaving. Or worrying more than we need to. We have to stick together and make it through the winter. It's strange, but if you ask me, the snow has made people calmer. Almost everyone was there when it was time to bring in the stove wood. I'll be bringing you some soon.

A prisoner of my bed, I curse my fate. I would have loved to contribute and fell a few tall trees. Instead, I twist and turn in bed, my head in a vise and my legs in splints.

Meanwhile, Joseph adds, we keep watch over the entrance to the village, but with this buildup of snow, I'd be surprised if we had any visitors. I'm happy not to have to do surveillance and carry my rifle wherever I go anymore. The thing is heavy for nothing. If there's a problem, the church bells will sound the alarm. That church has to be good for something. Jude asked us to go through the abandoned houses and gather up the supplies that people left behind. In one cellar, we found someone's garden harvest – potatoes, carrots, and turnips.

With those words, Joseph picks up the bag and sets it on the table. Matthias reaches for it immediately, delighted by the abundant manna.

And someone managed to dig up an old short-wave radio kit and solar panels, Joseph says.

Were you able to communicate with other villages? Matthias questions him.

No. We tried, but no one really knows how to use that thing. On the other hand, with the solar panels we can recharge our batteries without starting up the generators. And I found a hand-powered water pump. We drove a pipe into the snow and we can finally draw water directly from the river. We also came across some propane tanks, fondue pots, tools, and blankets. Some people use the search to take all the money they can find, as if the return of the electricity would usher in their hour of glory. There were a few skirmishes, but no one wanted to get involved.

Did you bring some milk? Matthias interrupts him.

No, that will be next time. There are only twelve cows left in the stable. All the rest turned into meat. The herd would not have made it through the winter with the hay we have. To go looking for milk is complicated, so we keep it for the children. But everyone who tasted your cheese really liked it. Some of them are ready to barter to get more.

Matthias raises his eyes and gives Joseph a questioning look.

I'm telling you, your cheese really is good. You should go see Jacques. He lives in the old hunting and fishing store. He's an odd duck, but his offers are always the best. Everyone ends up doing business with him.

Matthias thinks it over a moment, then goes back to

methodically putting away the meat, vegetables, and preserves. Joseph comes over to me.

It's good, you're getting stronger, or at least it looks that way to me. In the village nobody believes me when I say you're going to make it. While we're at it, I have a present for you. A while back I went and had a look at the old mine entrance. I hadn't been inside for fifteen years. Remember? We went there all the time when we were kids. I'd heard that people had holed up in there looking for shelter. But there was no one, that was just a rumour. Anyway, what can anyone do in that place? I mean, besides sneaking a cigarette, scaring the bats by shooting at them, and drawing timeless pictures of extinct animals on the walls? You remember, don't you?

Then Joseph slips his hand into the inside pocket of his coat and hands me a little box.

I stumbled over this in there.

As I am about to open it, I notice Matthias watching us on the sly as he divides up the rest of the supplies in the cellar. In the box, I discover a slingshot and a few iron pellets. I pick it up, test the elasticity of the rubber band, weigh the pellet in my hand, and place it in the middle of the leather band. I aim at different objects in the room, but don't dare take a shot. Joseph smiles.

I knew you'd like it. We had the same kind back in the day. Next time we'll see which one of us can still hit a target, but right now I have to go if I want to be back in the village before dark. Oh, I forgot, Maria says she'll come see you in the next few days.

As Joseph puts his coat back on and chats with Matthias, I practice with the slingshot, thinking of my uncles in the heart of the forest, living off the hunt.

Joseph says goodbye and closes the door. Suddenly the room seems empty. On the floor, his boot prints shine like great interlocking lakes seen from a mountain top at dawn.

Outside, shadows lengthen over the landscape. The wind has risen. I can hear it swoop down the stovepipe. The snow is heavy now. The flakes are so big that a single one could blot out the view. Matthias lights the oil lamp and, his eyes shining, holds up a package of meat high in the air like a trophy, like precious spoils.

So, hungry now?

SEVENTY-ONE

The squall shakes the porch, the walls groan, and the silence shatters clean through.

Matthias is sleeping. His breathing blends in with the flames growling in the woodstove. And the gusts of wind trapped under the eaves. Sleep eludes me. I think of Maria, the way she speaks to me, the way she laughs at my silence, her hands gentle when she examines my wounds, and the memories that well up when I see her. She hasn't come to see me for a long time. Time heals what it can, but nothing has been resolved. I am still lying here, and I watch the days leading one into the other and hope one day that my legs will carry me again. Meanwhile, Matthias feeds and cares for me. I know he has no choice. We are each other's prisoners.

Between two gusts of wind, I hear another sound. I think it is coming from the other side. Some small animal slipping along the wall in search of a way into our cellar. A mouse, maybe, or an ermine or a squirrel. Or something bigger, I can't tell.

I raise myself onto my elbows and look around the room, but the darkness is complete. I can't even make out Matthias on the sofa. In the depths of the night, only the red maw of the woodstove is visible.

The snow finally let up a few hours ago, at the end of the afternoon. The sky has lifted and the line of trees has become visible again, clear and imposing. With my spyglass, I examine the landscape to see if someone might be coming our way, but I spot only trees weighed down by snow. Beneath the branches are an infinite number of tunnels leading toward the mountains; those passageways are shored up by columns of stoic sap. The forest is a vault, vast and alive. I understand my aunts and uncles who have stayed there.

At this time of day, they must be debating one thing or another in their loud voices around the stove. The disorder of their words laid one on top of the other and their exclamations are the fruit of the alcohol they have not forgotten to bring, the precious rations that keep them warm. They talk about the day's hunt, or maybe stories from years past. They tease, they cut each other off, they start all over again. That's how it is. How it's always been. A storm of stories and jokes and laughter that makes the winter easier to bear.

Here the snow piles up in silence as Matthias cooks and cleans and I lose myself in the landscape. Here life is measured by supply days and nursing days. Here I cannot escape my bed and my wood splints.

Water is boiling in a big pot. Matthias gets up and pours it into the plastic basin. He sets the steaming receptacle on the edge of the table, and with a bar of soap and a sponge in his hand he comes at me.

Get undressed, it's bath time.

One by one I pull off my sweaters. But my T-shirt sticks to my skin and I get caught in one of them. Before finally coming to my rescue, Matthias watches me struggle uselessly. Then he pushes aside the blankets and rolls me onto one side to remove my underwear. Since he can't slide it down my legs because of my splints, he cuts it along one side. That way, he can take it off and put it back on afterward much more easily. Practical for him, but embarrassing for me.

I am naked on the edge of the bed. I feel my bones pushing against my flesh. Matthias moves the rocking chair over and puts his arms around my waist.

Come on now.

I grab onto his neck. His arms tighten, he grasps me to his chest and carries me to the rocking chair. When he sets me down, pain travels from my tibias to my jawbone. I try to concentrate on the cold drafts blowing across my skin. Matthias soaks the sponge in soapy water and hands it to me.

At least this way, if Maria comes calling in the next few days, you'll be cleaner, he jokes.

We size each other up a moment, then I look down at my splints. They are like hollow tree trunks, eaten away by ants.

Matthias sighs and shakes his head.

You know, sooner or later I'm going to make you talk. One way or another.

I wash myself the best I can, my arms, my armpits, between my legs. The sponge quickly cools off and the water evaporates off my body, carrying with it what little heat I have. I go as fast as I can. I clean my neck and face. My body shivers and goosebumps break out everywhere. I cough to let Matthias know I have finished. He takes over and rubs my back, thighs, and feet. He is brusque, rough but efficient. When he finishes, he hands me my sweater, then helps me put on a new pair of cut underwear.

I feel better sitting on the chair. Still as frail, maybe, but in better spirits. Matthias hands me a glass of water and some pills. They don't look the same colour as the usual ones. I don't care. I grab them and swallow them down.

Before putting me back in bed, Matthias washes himself in the same water. From the corner of one eye, I see him unlace his shoes, unbutton his sweater, and pull off his pants. He turns his back. Lit by the wavering light of the oil lamp, his silhouette is diaphanous. Even if he is well built and moves quicker than I do, his buttocks droop and his vertebrae press against his skin. I watch him scrub away at his bony body, rinse off quickly, and throw his clothes back on. The click of his belt buckle rattles in the room. When he moves to the mirror to smooth his hair, he stands still a moment, facing his reflection. He mutters something, but I can't make out what he is saying. A prayer, an incantation, or a sob.

When he turns around, I close my eyes and my neck muscles relax, as if I had drifted off.

Matthias takes a few steps in my direction.

You'll see, it won't be long with the pills you took – you won't have to pretend you're sleeping. You really will be quiet.

I am walking on a path of cracked earth and roots. The sun is beating down on the forest, the air is hot, and everything is dry. All around the trees press in, opaque and spiny. I am carrying a big bag on my back, yet it is weightless. Hidden in the branches, birds call to each other. Their song is clear, but I can't recognize the species. Squirrels dart across the path. There are many of them, and they are bold. They stop and examine me, crying out on their strident voices. I try to pay them no mind. My pace is good. Self-assured and vigorous. Suddenly the surroundings grow dark. The birds take flight, the squirrels huddle in their hiding places, the other animals slip into the underbrush. I move faster now. I have no idea what is happening. The wind rises and blows from every direction. The forest has turned on its head. I move faster still. Suddenly I smell smoke. I don't know where it is coming from. I spot a tall cedar a hundred metres off. I drop my bag and reach the tree by jumping over the roots that try to grab my ankles. The cedar is huge and its trunk lifts high into the sky. I grab onto its fibrous bark and climb as far up as I can. Everywhere is the smell of burned fibre, metal heated white hot, and charred flesh. When I can finally see over the crests of the pines in their close ranks, I see immense flames, swollen with pride and desire. They move forward, their step heavy, they laugh twisted laughter and devour the forest with an insatiable appetite.

I sit up in bed as if emerging from a coma. My dream scatters immediately, but my eyes and throat are stinging. My lungs are burning. In the dazzling light of day, a thick cloud of smoke whirls through the room.

I look around. Matthias is nowhere in sight. I am having trouble breathing. I cover my mouth with the edge of the sheet. Smoke is billowing from a pot on the stove like an erupting volcano.

I stir into action. I consider easing myself out of the bed, but I will never be able to lift myself up to reach the pot. Or open the door. But I have to get out of here! And in a hurry. Get out or do something. Do something or call for help. That's it, call for help. I have no choice.

Fire! Fire!

A few seconds later, the door to the other side swings open and Matthias runs into the room, through the spiralling smoke.

He moves to the stove, picks up the first piece of cloth he sees, grabs the pot, and rushes outside.

The smoke dissipates, driven out by the cold drafts of air. The room stinks, but at least we can breathe again. Matthias stands frozen in the doorway, staring at the sweater he picked up to protect his hand. The wool has been burned through in several places by the red-hot metal.

My wife gave me this sweater, he says in a shaky voice. I never wore it much, but I take it wherever I go.

The barometer points skyward and daylight floods the room. I lie in the sun the way cold-blooded animals do.

Ever since he forced me to call *Fire! Fire!* Matthias has not stopped pressing his advantage.

The neighbour lady never came, and your aunts and uncles left you here. We are alone in this world. But at least now you're talking. I know it's true, I heard you. I always knew you'd end up giving in.

Suddenly, the sound of a motor in the distance. Matthias freezes, as if he had heard the cry of an animal that has been extinct for millions of years. I get out my spyglass and scan the horizon. A yellow snowmobile appears at the top of the hill. It is pulling a sled piled high with wood. The driver is standing, head lowered, both hands gripping the controls. I lose him behind some trees, but the noise of the clattering pistons comes closer. The yellow snowmobile speeds into sight, then halts by the front door. It's Joseph with his load of wood. Matthias hurries to open the door.

Smells like smoke here, Joseph says.

Matthias dodges the subject and asks him how he managed to find some gas. Joseph leans against the door frame. His eyes are shining.

I didn't have to convince anyone, you know.

Matthias pitches in to unload the wood. When they finish they come inside to warm up and drink coffee. Joseph figures we can heat the place for quite a while with what he brought. Not all the way to spring, but almost. But there's some green birch in the lot, he warns us.

You'll see, some of the logs will hiss.

He pulls out a metal flask and pours some brownish alcohol into his coffee. Then he inquires after Maria.

I bet José was with her when she came. He'd follow her everywhere if he could.

Matthias and I look at each other.

We haven't seen Maria in a long time, Matthias says.

Really, Joseph says, surprised, that's strange. Everything's quiet in the village. I'm going to go see her, he decides, turning up the collar of his coat. If José lets me. You know, it's never easy with guys like him.

Then Joseph drinks off the rest of his coffee, wishes us well, and climbs onto his snowmobile. Before he starts it, Matthias runs out to remind him not to forget to bring milk next time. For cheese. Joseph nods, pulls on the crank, and damages the landscape by revving up the engine.

Meanwhile, in the woodstove, the green logs whistle in the flames as if cursing their fate.

Today, everything is grey. The snow and the sky run together. Only the black triangle of the tall spruce trees hints at the horizon.

Matthias has gone out. With my spyglass, I watch him trudging ahead, fighting the snow. More than once he stops to catch his breath, then sets out again with a determined step. Further on, in the folds of the landscape, I spot another figure. The person is wearing a bright red coat and moving quickly, as if she were gliding over the snow. When Matthias sees her, he waves. They move toward each other and come together in the clearing, near the snow gauge. I watch them talk a moment, then they turn toward the house.

A short time later the door opens and Matthias comes in with Maria. As he shakes off his snowshoes, she leans her cross-country skis against the wall and unbuttons her coat. I try to sit up in bed in as dignified a way as possible.

How are you doing? she asks.

I go to answer, but Matthias cuts in first.

He'll make it, he says, he'll make it.

Joseph told me you're doing better, Maria pursues, looking me in the eye, and I see he's right. Can I examine you?

I nod. She comes closer, acknowledging my smile, then puts down the bag she was wearing across her body. When she leans over to place her hand on my forehead, I can sense the shape of her breasts beneath her sweater.

I would like to thank her. Tell her I'm happy to see her, that I remember her, back when she was young, when we were in school together. Tell her how beautiful a woman she has become, that her wavy hair and delicate features and the ease of her gestures would bring a dying man back to life. But when I open my mouth to speak, she sticks a thermometer into it.

Keep it under your tongue and close your lips around it.

Then she uncovers my legs and loosens my splints. Matthias joins her.

José isn't with you? he asks.

No, José isn't with me. Jenny is going to give birth any day now. He stayed behind with the family. In case the contractions begin.

While she unwraps the gauze, I stare at the ceiling beams. It is the only way to stay calm. And keep pain at a distance. I feel ridiculous with my injuries, my silence, and my underwear that fasten on the side. I know my legs are covered with bruises, and my thighs and calves are atrophied. I know I look more like a ghost than a man.

Did Joseph come and see you? Matthias asks.

No. I mean yes, he came by, Maria says, blushing.

Then she palpates my bones, bends my knees, and gently turns my ankles. Her hands are warm and attentive. Pain rises in me, along with desire.

You're experiencing pain, and that's normal, she tells me, because of your ligaments. Still, we should cut back on the analgesics because sooner or later you're going to have to get used to the feeling. Your right leg is healing well, but the left is recuperating more slowly.

Suddenly I remember what Matthias told me at the beginning to frighten me. And force me to accept his care.

You see that? he shouted, pointing to the handsaw hanging on the wall, that's what's awaiting you. We're living like the old-time lumberjacks in the camps. A cabin buried by the snow, a woodstove, just enough to survive on. Their techniques are ours too. When the axe slipped from a man's hand because of cold, fatigue, or overreaching, and it sunk deep into his thigh or tibia or foot, there was only one solution. Brandy, fire, and the saw. Otherwise it was gangrene, fever, and a horribly slow death.

As I gaze at the handsaw hanging on the wall, Maria takes out my stitches one by one, using tweezers and a pair of scissors.

She works gently, but I can feel my flesh pulling. I turn toward her.

It'll be all right, she tells me, her eyes focused, I'm almost finished.

As she rewraps my bandages, Maria asks me how I feel. I make a few unintelligible sounds. She laughs and takes the thermometer out of my mouth. She had forgotten all about it.

I'm okay, I tell her, looking at the immaculate whiteness of my new bandages. I'll be all right.

When he hears my voice, Matthias lifts his head.

In any case your fever is gone, Maria says.

When am I going to be able to walk?

Be patient, she tells me. Your bones are knitting well, but your muscles are still very weak. Start by taking off your splints from time to time. That'll do you good.

Then she gives me a wink and turns and hands Matthias her bag.

Take this. There's fresh gauze, ointment, antibiotics, and everything else you'll need. Some of it is past the expiry date, but that doesn't matter.

I'm making soup. Why don't you stay and eat with us?

Thank you, she declines, but I really must go. I'm expected in the village. I'll be back soon.

Everyone says the same thing around here, Matthias mutters.

Maria smiles, but says no more, takes her skis and goes out the door. Through the window, the red stain of her coat grows fainter, giving light to the landscape.

Matthias puts the soup on the stove and shakes the fire with a poker. When he turns in my direction, his pupils are the colour of burning embers.

EIGHTY-ONE

Matthias carries a chair to my bedside and sets up the chess game on my table.

I smile, but would rather play cards, maybe even for money.

I always knew you'd end up giving in, he goes back to his old refrain. If we can't change things, we can always change the words that describe them. I'm not your doctor, I'm not your friend, and I'm not your father, understand? We're spending the winter here, we have to get through it, and then it's finished. I'm looking after you, and we're sharing everything, but as soon as I can leave, you'll forget about me. You'll get along on your own. I'm going back to the city. Understand? My wife is waiting for me. She needs me and I need her. That's my adventure, that's my life, I have nothing to do here, this is all a big accident, a twist of fate, a terrible mistake.

He says that, then moves a piece on the chessboard and dares me to challenge him.

I always knew you'd end up giving in. No one can keep his mouth shut like that. Everyone turns back to words sooner or later. Even you. And soon, I'm telling you, you're going to speak to me. You're going to talk to me, even without a fire in a pot, even if I'm not a young veterinarian. You're going to talk to me, understand? And you're going to play chess with me. That's what's going to happen. That and no more. Now go ahead, it's your move.

III. ICARUS

If you fly too low, the humidity will weigh upon your plumage and you will crash to the ground. If you fly too high, the heat of the sun will break your wings apart and you will plummet into emptiness. I've taught you that lesson twice, ten times, a hundred times. Because at your age, everyone thinks they are invincible. Maybe you think I'm old and a wet blanket, but remember that I know what you don't. Once we take flight from this lifeless, hermetic place, you will gaze in wonder at the depth of the horizon. By then we will be far from here. By then we will be saved.

EIGHTY-FOUR

The icicles hanging from the roofline cut the landscape into vertical planes. The snow reflects the clear blue sky. The cold has stiffened the pine needles. A few flakes wander between sky and earth. I don't know where they come from. They are carried on the wind, and never touch the ground. Like meteors going by at close range, but never reaching us.

Matthias does his calisthenics. He jumps up and down in place. His limbs are loose and his slender old body reacts to the impact with impressive flexibility. When he strikes his chest with the palm of his hand, the cavernous depth of his lungs is audible.

I watch him go through his paces and figure I am getting better. Soon I will be able to get out of bed. Pain is still a close companion, like a sleeping animal, but I have stopped needing pills to tolerate its presence by my side.

When he finishes his exercises, Matthias opens the trap door to the cellar and takes out some food.

I can give you a hand, I tell him.

He looks up. Hesitates. Maybe he thinks I want to deprive him of the privilege of passing the time by preparing the meals, but he ends up accepting.

Here, he says, bringing me a knife and a cutting board, take care of the vegetables for the soup, I'll make the bread.

As I peel potatoes, I realize this is the first time I have made myself useful since I came here. I still can't stand up and I'm not very skillful when it comes to cooking, but at least I'm doing something. Meanwhile, Matthias kneads the dough and whistles, though he really only pushes air through the spaces between his teeth. Maybe he is imitating the sound of rivers swollen with spring run-off. Or the icy wind whirling above our porch room.

As the soup simmers, the steam that rises into the air sticks to my window. With the cold outside, it forms a fine layer of frost. To see through I have to scratch an opening in the glass. A little porthole in the stained glass of crystals. As I look outside, Matthias tells me his father was a cook in the lumber camps. And that he was his assistant for a few years, after the end of the war.

I remember they used to leave once the rivers hit flood stage. Plenty of them were willing to brave the fast waters to drive the logs to the mills. None of them could swim, no one wore a life jacket, but all of them had a cross around their necks. They rode the floating logs with their hobnailed boots, their staff, and their songs. When a log-driver got swallowed up by the water and disappeared between the trunks, he could trust only his prayers. Sometimes his brothers managed to fish out his body before it got swept away by the current, but most of the time the rapids and the freezing water left no chance. Every evening, when they sat down at the table, they would reflect a moment, then eat everything set before them as if it was their last supper.

As the slabs of black bread cook on the stove and the scent of grilling flour fills the room, Matthias points toward the crucifix he hung above the front door.

I lift my eyebrows.

It's ready, he says.

He serves us the soup and breaks a slab of bread in two. It's hot, and steaming inside. I dip it into the soup and bite into it with gusto. As he recites some kind of grace, I challenge him with my mouth full.

We're like the log-drivers you talk about. Only we don't need a crucifix, we need a horseshoe.

Matthias stares at me a moment as if I didn't understand. Then, slowly, his face brightens and he thanks me for sharing his daily bread.

Matthias helps me get to the rocking chair. Again, I am surprised by his strength when he holds me up. But I suppose I have never been so light, so frail.

I am sitting by the stove with my spyglass and a blanket. Matthias is close at hand, at the table. He threads a needle.

I have a new angle on the landscape. I still see the forest that stands without compromise above the snow. But from this point of view, I can make out the poles and electric wires that cross the fields and link us to the village. Those metal cables on which our lives were once suspended. Those conduits were invested with mysterious power. Those black lines on which a few birds are perched as if nothing had changed.

The sun is setting and the cold turns yesterday's snow into a dazzling sheet. When I close my eyes, I see colours that don't exist. When I open them, it is so bright I feel like I'm suffering from snow blindness.

As he darns a pair of jeans, Matthias asks me what I did before the blackout. He knows the answer, I'm sure.

I was a mechanic.

Like your father?

Yes, like my father.

And since the blackout, do you still consider yourself a mechanic?

I hold my breath a moment, and look at my hands, then my legs. With the accident and the power outage, all the time I spent underneath vehicles, my hands in oil and iron filings, is just a vague memory.

As he carefully ties off the thread, Matthias states that for him nothing has changed. He earned his living doing all sorts of things, and he has been married fifty-seven years.

I've always managed to get by. One more winter is not going to make a difference.

On those words, he sticks himself with the needle. He jumps to his feet, goes to the window, and changes the subject.

We're going to have snow, he predicts, I can feel it.

For the moment, the sky is completely clear. I look out at the barometer and see the little branch pointing up, no hesitation there.

With his lips, Matthias sucks off the blood that blossoms like a pearl on his fingertip. I wonder if he understands what is happening. What is becoming of us. What awaits us. Maybe he has not grasped the magnitude of the blackout.

Unless I'm the one who's completely lost his grip.

Matthias was wrong, it didn't snow. Soon it will be a week since we saw our last cloud. During the day, sunlight fills the porch, and at night, stars pierce the sky. Only the blowing snow gives the impression that the white blanket has thickened in places.

We play chess and talk about this and that. The winter, food, my legs. Our conversations are sporadic since our games require all our attention. I still have not managed to beat him, but I am beginning to learn his tactics, his reflexes, his habits, and he knows it. He has stopped leaving anything to chance. He makes minute calculations before moving the slightest pawn. As if a reversal of fortune were something inconceivable.

It is my move when suddenly someone knocks on the door. Matthias jumps to his feet and orders me not to touch anything.

A man is standing in the doorway overflowing with light. Jonas. I have not seen him for over ten years, but I recognize him the moment he sets foot in the room. When I worked at my father's garage, we used to see him going by on his bike. He always looked drunk, though he never touched a drop. He whistled and sang as he zigzagged along on his bicycle. Every day, in his innocence, he rummaged through roadside ditches and garbage cans in search of empty beer bottles. Often we saw him along the road, gathering up bottles and talking to himself

out loud. From a distance, it looked as if he v
with the horizon.

He is wearing snow pants patched at the k
coat, a fur cap, and a long yellow scarf. An
pair of crutches. He comes in and leans them
He sits down on the stool, breathing hard. H
with effort and cold.

It's not easy, it's hard getting anywhere with all this snow, he says, stumbling over his words. With snowshoes on my feet, I'm always afraid I'll fall down and not be able to get up. I needed, it took me an hour to get here, maybe more.

Matthias seems surprised by this unexpected visit, but Jonas does not give it any thought. He watches me, his face split by a big smile.

I remember when you were no higher than that. When you came up to here. You used to run through the village with the kids your age. You tried to scare me. Scare me when I was out hunting empties.

Jonas has gotten older, but has not really changed. He moves the same way, hesitant but abrupt. The same overstated enthusiasm. The same luminous emptiness in his eyes. It's true, he practically doesn't have a hair on his head anymore, or a tooth in his mouth, but the way he speaks is just as fast. Sometimes his words pile up and fall over each other. As if he were in a hurry to speak his piece, in case it changed before he could get it out.

I didn't know it was you they found underneath the car wreck last summer. Had I known. Had I known I would have come and visited. To tell you I'm sorry about your father. Yes, sorry. He wasn't doing very well. In the village people said all kinds of things about him. People are like that. I should, I should know. I remember him well, I used to go see him at the garage all the time, I used to sit in a corner and talk to him as he worked. You left the village and you didn't come back. Lots of water, that's

of water under the bridge now. My poor mother died too.
t she was luckier, she went before the blackout happened.

Matthias puts the soup on the stove. I search for something to say. My father, his poor mother, the blackout. That's how it is, nothing to be done.

It's nice of you to come, I end up telling him.

Pretty Maria told me you were here, he says. She gave me a pair of crutches for you. Look. She asked me to bring them for you. They're real crutches. Real wood crutches. I wanted to bring them before, but yesterday a kid from the village came back from the forest with his face all bloody. Jacob. He was crying and nobody could understand a thing, not a word of what he was saying.

Jonas blinks his eyes hard a few times, then swallows his spit and goes back to his story.

When it happened he was bleeding a lot. They cleaned off his face, but there was nothing, nothing anyone could do. People started to panic. I wasn't doing anything, so they asked me to go for help. So that's what I did. Maria wasn't at home. José opened the door. I told him everything and he went right away. I kept on looking, because Maria is the one who takes care of hurt people usually. But she wasn't anywhere. So I knocked at Joseph's place. He came to the door half-naked, like he'd just gotten out of bed. I told him everything that happened. I was just finishing my story when pretty Maria came up behind him, buttoning her shirt in a hurry. She thanked me, got her coat, and went right out. I stood there a moment in the doorway with Joseph. It was cold, but that didn't seem to bother him. He looked me in the eye and made me promise not to say a word. I promised because it looked very, very important.

From the corner of my eye, I spot Matthias smiling, as if he had won a bet.

When I found Jacob again, Maria and José were fixing his wounds. In the meantime, he told what happened. He captured an ermine by trapping it in a hollow log. When he bent over to look at it, it leapt at his face. Those little beasts are nasty. You have to take care. Especially if they feel trapped. They're completely white with a pink muzzle. They're pretty, but nasty. Jacob got his cheek and his eyebrow cut up. Nothing, nothing too bad. But what a morning! That's why, that's why I didn't come and bring you the crutches yesterday. Because of Jacob. And the ermine.

Matthias hands a bowl of soup to Jonas, who accepts it gladly.

Two days from now, there's going to be a dance in the village, Jonas announces between two gulps. Jude is organizing it in the church basement. With generators and everything. He says there's going to be beer and a hot meal. He's been talking about it forever, and everyone, everyone is invited. I'll be there, you can count on that. For the hot meal and the empties. Nobody wants to buy them from me anymore, but I put them aside. One day, one day I'll go get the deposit and that'll give me some money. A lot of money.

Jonas empties his bowl noisily by drinking directly from it, then he sets it down on the table with a look of satisfaction.

It's going to snow pretty soon, he claims. The clouds, the clouds are like horse tails. It's cold, but you can feel the humidity in the air. And the wind is going to blow for the next few days, that's for sure. But you're all right here. With the sun and the stove, you're better off, much better than on the other side, right?

Matthias nods as Jonas gets up, puts his coat, his fur cap, and scarf back on.

I've got to go back down to the village. I promised, I promised to help out in the stable this afternoon. We're going to get the hay out of the loft. That's a lot of snowshoeing for one day and I don't like walking with these things on my feet. But that's all right, I'm happy to see you, see you again. After all, this place is your place. And the crutches, the crutches that pretty Maria found for you, they're right there. You know, I remember when you were yay-high. You ran through the village with the other kids your age. You tried to scare me. But it never worked. No, never. Maybe you heard me from the distance, but I saw you coming. I always saw you coming.

Thanks for the crutches, I can't wait to use them.

I remember, I always saw you coming, Jonas says one last time, and closes the door behind him.

We hear him continuing his conversation as he moves off. Through the window, I watch him head down toward the village with his gesticulations and his patchwork clothes. Matthias goes back to his spot in the rocking chair and stares intently at the chessboard.

I look at the barometer that seems to be pointing downward despite the clear skies. I think of the dance that will take place the day after tomorrow. I envy Jonas for being able to attend. If only I could walk, I would go too. I wouldn't dance until I'd had more than enough to drink, but before that I'd see a few familiar faces, I'd find out a little more about what was happening in the village, and I'd talk about things with Maria and try to make her laugh.

Go ahead, it's your turn, Matthias says impatiently. Go ahead and play, and get it over with.

NINETY-SIX

It has been snowing for two days. The mountains that curve above the village and the line of the forest have disappeared from sight. The snow hurries to reach the earth and the immensity of the landscape has narrowed down to the four walls of this room.

Matthias is sitting in the rocking chair, absorbed in a book that he found on the other side. The afternoon will pass this way. He turns a page from time to time, and I watch the landscape swallow us up in slow motion. The wind rises as night falls. Squalls shake the trees and sweep past the porch. Jonas had it right. First snow, then wind.

Later, Matthias puts down his book and goes over to the stove. He stirs the soup and stares down at the bottom of the kettle.

Stories always repeat, he says after a time. We wanted to escape the fate that was assigned us and here we are, swallowed up by life's course. Gulped down by a whale. Far from the surface, we hope it will spit us back up on the shore. We are in the belly of winter, in its very entrails. In this warm darkness, we know we can't escape what will befall us.

Night has fallen. The snow keeps falling, but it has taken on shadows. Strange, but a weak glow illuminates the bottom edge of the sky. As if they had lit a streetlamp in the village. I observe the yellowish ring with my spyglass. A vague halo through the crests of the trees, and snowflakes harried by the wind.

Matthias lights the oil lamp and serves the soup.

As I empty my bowl, I realize that the light in the sky has become brighter. The village streets seem illuminated. We can hear the church bells. They must be celebrating the dance. I would have loved to be there and believe, if only for a few hours, that life is normal again.

The snow and the wind dropped off suddenly this morning. Like an animal that, for no apparent reason, gives up one prey to hunt another. Dense and heavy, the silence surprised us, since we still feared the gusts would tear off the roof and suck us up into emptiness.

When we look out the window, it is like gazing on the open sea. On all sides, the wind has sculpted giant waves of snow that froze just as they were about to wash over us.

With calmer weather, Matthias decides to take a look outside. In the endless tunnel of my spyglass, I watch him disappear across the snow hardened by the cold. His form grows fainter as he reaches the forest. He is like one of the Three Kings moving toward his star.

There are three tin cans on the counter. Open and empty. I take out my slingshot and a few iron pellets. I extend my arm, aim, and pull back the rubber band. When I let it go, the pellet cuts through the air with a whistling sound, misses its target, bounces off the wall, and ends up buried in the pile of logs by the stove. I start over. This time, I make sure my wrist is lined up straight with my arm. I close one eye and fire. One of the tin cans rattles to the floor. Not the one I was aiming for. But I still have some pellets.

Matthias returns from his walk with an armful of wood.

When you see the house from a distance, he says, taking off his coat, you realize how much snow is piled up on the roof. It's absolutely crazy.

As he kneels down in front of the stove, he spots the tin cans upended on the floor. He looks in my direction. I display my slingshot. He smiles and sets up the metal targets on the counter again.

Go ahead, he challenges me, show me what you can do.

Dawn has broken. The sun has not yet risen, but the sky is bright. The snow glitters. We are drinking coffee. Even if it tastes very much like yesterday's version, we hold onto our cups jealously and savour it, one sip at a time.

The porch is adapting to the cold. The wood structure has stiffened. The foundations clench their teeth. Sometimes, sharp tinkling noises echo between the beams: roofing nails yielding under pressure. The village chimneys give off generous amounts of smoke. Under every roof people are awakened by the icy caress of winter and they hurry to get the fire going again. Birch bark produces white smoke that rises straight through the still air. Like marble columns holding up the sky. As if we were living in a cathedral.

Once he has finished his lengthy contemplation, Matthias gulps down the rest of his coffee, turns away from the window, and begins his exercises. He balances on one leg, one arm stretched toward the ceiling, the other flat on his stomach. He rolls his shoulders and loosens his muscles, then squats down and straightens several times. I watch him go through his paces and tell myself that though my body is regenerating a little more each day, he is the one with new blood in his veins.

Suddenly the door swings open and Joseph appears on the threshold in a great cloud of steam. With his smoking nostrils and his loaded sled, he looks like a draft horse, shining with labour. His beard is frosted over and icicles hang from his moustache. He frees himself from his harness, sits down, takes off his mittens, and blows on his hands. He tries to take off his coat but his fingers are paralyzed by the biting cold and he cannot work his zipper.

Matthias heats up oatmeal and begins unloading the wood Joseph has brought us.

You know, Joseph tells us, Jude organized a dance last week. He started up the generators. Everyone was there. You could hear the music everywhere in the village. It was a party, just perfect. Like in a dream. People were eating and dancing. When the church bells rang in the middle of the night, they thought it was a joke. But someone cut the music and said there was a chimney fire in a house next door. When we got there, it was too late. The wind rose and whipped up the flames and the roof caught. Smoke came whirling out of the windows. The church bells were still ringing away, but we couldn't hear them because of the wind. We waited and watched the fire. The gusts of wind pushed the heat into our faces. The flames wrapped around the gables and the beams. The sky was orange above our heads, as if the streets were lit the way they used to be. The snow was melting and streams of water were rushing past our feet. We were sure the house would burn to the ground. But the flames decided to devour part of the roof and the upstairs. As if they were toying with us. The next day, the house was still smoking, but there was nothing more to see. Just the charred rafters that were still hissing.

What about the people? Matthias asks, glancing up at the spot where the stove's chimney climbs up past the ceiling.

At first, Joseph tells him, we were afraid for them. But luckily there was no one in the house when the fire broke out. In the days afterward, we found them new lodgings. But when they went back to recover their things, everything they owned was black and stunk of smoke. You know that kind of sticky, greasy smoke. Since then we've swept most of the chimneys in the village. With how cold it's been these last days, people are burning whatever they can. Sometimes they lose control and the stoves overheat.

Joseph pauses, then runs his hand slowly over his forehead and his eyes.

During the last snowstorm, someone stole Jude's snowmobile. At first José accused me but, you know, that made no sense. Later they realized that Jérémie had disappeared with his nine-year-old son. Everybody wanted to hunt them down, but the snow had covered their tracks long before. They tried comforting Jérémie's wife instead, but she was inconsolable. José gave her some sleeping pills. All I hope is that Jérémie took enough gas to get somewhere. No one wants to imagine how Jude will react if he ever sets foot here again.

Matthias offers Joseph a bowl of oatmeal, which he gladly accepts.

And then, he continues, a number of people have fallen sick lately. Some got better on their own, you know, but others can't seem to find their way back to health. Including Judith who took over schooling the children after Jean refused to do it anymore. Maria does what she can to help them, but she's not a magician.

Joseph shovels the food into his mouth. A few oat flakes stick to his moustache.

You're better off here, he concludes. Away from all that.

Matthias interrupts to ask him if he managed to get any milk. Joseph smiles.

Yes, I went to the stable this morning. While everyone was still in bed. The stable's not heated, and I'm always surprised how comfortable it is in there. You know cows produce the heat they need. I could have stretched out and finished my night's sleep. But Jonas was sleeping on the hay bales. He woke up as I was milking a cow. He was surprised to see me, but I told him to act like I wasn't there, and he went back to sleep.

Matthias peers into the sacks of food and takes out two large containers of milk. He opens one and samples it.

It's really fresh, he says, wiping his mouth on his sleeve. It's perfect, thanks.

The families living in the notary's old house made potted meat and fish pâtés, all kinds of things. I'll bring you some. Might as well enjoy it. Even if we still have a good stock of food in the village, people are strict about rationing. Jude insists on being careful. And then there's a rumour that the people in a village along the coast were able to hook up to a windmill. Everyone's talking about it, everybody has an opinion. It could be true. There's no electricity here, but on the sides of the mountains those machines are still working. Some people say they're going to go there. On the other hand, if we believed what everyone says, the blackout would have been over a long time ago, and we should all be watching television with a cold beer and a TV dinner fresh out of the microwave.

Joseph sighs, then takes out his tobacco pouch. He rolls a cigarette, lights it, and inhales deeply. He goes on talking, but I have stopped paying attention. I follow the scrolls of smoke slowly issuing from his mouth.

You want one? he asks me.

With pleasure.

Joseph leans in my direction, surprised.

You talk now? That's great news!

I give him a smile.

We smoke as Matthias busies himself with sorting the food.

Any news from my uncles? I ask, my head spinning from the tobacco.

I went and had a look at their place, Joseph tells me. There are no vehicles in the garage, the canoes are gone, and every room was completely emptied. Your aunts and uncles took everything with them. Food, tools, clothing. Everything useful. But I found this, he adds, pulling a folded piece of paper from the inside pocket of his coat. It's a map of the region. It might prove useful.

I take it and thank him. I wonder if my aunts and uncles really intend to come back to the village. They might have left forever. Unless something happened to them.

Oh, I almost forgot the good news, Joseph adds. A woman gave birth in the village. Despite what some people feared, everything went normally. Maria was there. She's no magician, you know, but sometimes she can work miracles. She helped deliver a little girl, Joëlle. The first child of the blackout. No one knows who the father is, but Jenny, the mother, is staying in the house by the sawmill, it's big and there are a lot of people in there, so she's well looked after.

Joseph stands and buttons his coat.

Next time I'll get the snow off the roof, he promises. With everything that's accumulated up there, it must be getting pretty heavy.

Yes, Matthias tells him, I was going to ask you about that.

Remind me when I come back. Right now, though, I've got to go back down the hill. Maria is waiting. I promised I'd take her ice-fishing and today's the day.

Joseph waves goodbye and the door closes behind him as if slammed by a gust of wind.

Matthias finishes sorting the provisions Joseph brought. He glares at the prepared food. He mutters and grumbles that he's the cook here, but then he stows everything away carefully just the same.

It's true, he says after making his calculations, they've cut back on the rations.

He pours the milk into the kettle that we use to melt snow and places it on the stove.

It has to warm up. Warm up but not boil, he tells me as he adds rennet.

He stirs the mixture, then takes the pot off the fire.

Now we have to wait.

We play a few chess games and finish off the rest of the oatmeal. Matthias wins every one. I make fun of his skill by telling him I'm letting him beat me. He lifts his chin in my direction, squints, but says nothing.

He goes over to the stove and stirs the pot with a spoon. It smells like clotted milk. Then he pours the contents through a filter made of a metal hanger and a length of cloth. The whitish mixture begins draining slowly.

I don't let up.

I let you win every time. And you know it.

Matthias won't react. He allows himself the shadow of a

frown, and tells me I don't know what I'm talking about, my fever must have returned. I smile, then take out the map Joseph gave me.

I examine the gradient markers, the plateaus, the river beds. I pick out the coastal villages at the top of the map, then ours, surrounded by valleys. Further on is the lake where we fished when we were kids. The two main roads are clearly visible. The one that follows the coast, and the other that cuts through the interior. I can make out the dotted lines of the logging roads that push their way into the heart of the valleys. Here and there drawings of tall grass indicate swampy zones. All the rest is forest.

I look at the scale at the bottom.

It's enormous.

Certain sections of a river have been identified by hand. I remember having heard those names, but I can't tell them apart. My uncles' hunting camp must not be far, in a river bend, in the middle of the hundred-year-old cedars. I remember it very well, but I can't locate it on the map.

That's it, I say to myself, putting my finger on the little "x" sketched with a lead pencil. It's there.

When I look up, Matthias is still inspecting the contents of his operation.

The texture is just right, he says, satisfied. It's starting to look like cheese.

In the night, I heard the little animal again. I recognized its discreet footsteps, its furtive movements, and how it was interested in the food in the cellar. It would stop to listen carefully, then probably steal back to the other side with part of our provisions. It seems to be meticulously laying up a stock of reserves for the times to come.

At first light, Matthias disassembles his production. He presses the soft white mass to extract the water, adds salt, then makes six balls as big as his fist and flattens them with great care. On the stove, in an old pot, he melts some candle-ends. He watches the wax liquefy as he removes bits of wick and blackened matches. Then he pours the hot wax over the cheeses, making sure to cover them completely.

This is one of the best ways of keeping it, he tells me.

I nod and say nothing. Then look toward the chess game.

I don't have time, he answers. I have to go down to the village.

He carefully places the cheeses wrapped in wax in a cloth sack. He gives me a can of baked beans with a slab of black bread, loads the stove, and gets dressed quickly.

I'll see you later, he calls, putting on his snowshoes.

Then he hurries out of the room.

Outside, the snow is reaching hungrily for the earth.

It must be getting close to noon. At first the cold seemed to loosen its grip on the landscape, only to return with greater force. Meanwhile, snow keeps falling and nothing can stop it. The flakes are large and delicate. They look like they have been cut from paper.

In the stove the final embers are going out. I can feel the cold slipping under my window. The drafts have long icy hands and they move past me like shades that want to reach under my blankets.

Maria said I will be able to stand up soon. My left leg is still fragile, but with crutches I should be able to move around by myself. The next time she comes, I will go to the door to welcome her.

First I sit up straight, then slide to the edge of the bed. My legs hang uselessly. I think of my next move and contemplate the precipice before me. Gravity pulls me toward the floor. In the prison of their splints, my thighs and calves have turned to stone in their immobility. My muscles hang off my bones like flesh that even scavengers don't want.

You are skinny and dried up. You weigh nothing at all. But you'll figure out how to take a few steps. You'll manage somehow, I tell myself out loud, you're still alive, so you've got no choice. You have to walk.

I could go as far as the chair. Or the sofa. The chair is closer, but the crutches are behind the sofa. I could make it, even if I have to hop on my right leg instead of putting one foot in front of the other.

I just have to slide down from the bed and try to lean on the table. Nothing to it. Just make sure not to lose my balance. It would be stupid to burn myself on the stove.

At first all that seems insurmountable and I consider lying back down. But then I take a deep breath, tighten my splints, and slip down to the floor. Slowly. Very slowly, like with the icy water of a lake at the beginning of summer.

My toes touch the floor. I grab firmly onto the bedsheets but they slide with me. I feel my heart pumping. My legs stiffen and electric current travels through the marrow of my bones. The blood flows heavily through my veins, running a painful circuit from my feet to my head. There, now I'm standing. I can shuffle my feet across the floor. Sweat breaks out on my forehead. The table is close by. Just steady your body long enough to get to the next support. I take a chance and put a little more weight on my left leg. I reach for the table. I'm almost there. I stretch further. I contain the pain. It's nothing, nothing to it. I steady myself. My hand is trembling as if I were trying to lift furniture with the sheer force of my thoughts. Suddenly I go numb. The chair stands kilometres away, behind the table. My sight is narrowed by thick black blotches. Then my knees let go.

The floor is dirty and cold. Dried mud, dust, pieces of bark, onion skins. The floorboards are grey beneath the chipped varnish. I don't know how long I have been lying here. A few minutes. A few hours. It's still light outside, but Matthias hasn't come back.

I can't stay like this, on the floor. I look around. I prop myself up on my elbows and crawl toward the sofa. My legs follow me like a long overcoat heavy with sludge. I make slow progress. I am sinking into the floor as I move. I keep watch over the door with the fearfulness of wild animals. The fear of being caught in a moment of vulnerability.

I don't want Maria to see me like this.

I reach the foot of the sofa. I am out of breath and my elbows hurt. It's hard, but I hoist myself up onto the threadbare cushions. I arrange my legs straight in front of me. Under the splint I see that the bandage on my left side is soaked with blood. I grab Matthias's quilt and cover the bottom half of my body with it.

I am empty. As if part of me was still back on the floor. Maybe I should eat something, but now the can of baked beans is too far away.

I close my eyes a moment.

And then nothingness.

I am startled awake. It is dark. Matthias puts a sack on the table, shakes the snow off his shoulders, and lights the oil lamp. When he looks around, he sees my bed is empty. His lower jaw tightens and a vein appears on his forehead. Then when he spots me lying on the sofa, he raises his eyes and walks over to me. He slips one arm around my back and the other behind my knees and carries me to my bed the way adults do with sleeping children. Or the dying. I try to hide my bloody bandage, but Matthias sees it right away. He says nothing, but he saw it. He pulls up my blankets and tells me to get some sleep, then disappears into the other side with a candle and the sack he put on the table.

I stare at the ceiling as if gazing down into an abyss. Pain is a bird of prey that holds me in its clutches.

I feel like I've taken one step forward. And two steps back.

Someone is standing on the front step. I sit up in bed. I look toward the sofa, then the rocking chair, but I don't see Matthias. I hear the click of the doorknob and Maria is there on the threshold. She smiles and comes to me. The morning sun fills the room as if time had stopped. I push aside my blankets, unfasten the splints, and leap to my feet. Her eyes illuminate the room. I move toward her, take off her red coat, and slip a hand around her waist. We kiss. Her mouth is warm. Our foreheads touch and our bodies entwine. I lift her gently, she clings to me, then we lie on the kitchen table. Our clothes fall to the floor with no resistance. She takes my hands and presses them against her hips, and moves them across her body. I kiss her neck, her skin is soft and a little salty. I kneel between her legs, impatient, energetic, full of desire. Our eyes thirst for each other. I take her, she bends to me, and nothing exists outside of us.

When I awake a kettle is simmering on the woodstove. It smells of meat and boiled vegetables. When he sees my eyes are open, Matthias moves the stool over and sits down in front of me as if we were about to begin a game of chess. But he is here to change my dressing.

I hide my erection under the blankets. My dream is very near, yet very far away. My left leg is giving me serious pain.

He unwraps my bandage, cleans the dried blood, disinfects

the wound, and wraps it up again with the butterfly bandages at hand.

You're lucky, the splint held your bones in place, Matthias grumbles.

Outside, the sun strikes the snow full on. The sky is cutting and the barometer reaches for it. Before my window the icicles look threatening and the snow keeps piling up. It is like a mouth closing around us.

I am completely exhausted. I feel like I will never stand up again. If winter doesn't get me, it will be something else. I can't do anything. Outside of a little repartee, looking out the window, and waiting. That doesn't give much to hang onto.

Matthias grabs the pair of crutches behind the sofa and orders me to get up.

Isn't that what you wanted? Then you'll have to build up your strength.

I consider the two pieces of wood stuck together with little metal brackets.

We're going to do some exercises.

Matthias lifts me up by the armpits.

Come on, you don't want it bad enough. You need strong arms to walk on crutches. Stand straight. Do what I do.

Matthias starts by rotating his head, stretching out his arms on both sides, and breathing deeply. I imitate him the best I can, sitting on the edge of my bed. He bends his elbows, clasps his hands behind his back, and leans his torso forward.

Hold the position, he explains. Hold it and extend it. You should feel your body, you should be centred on it, push harder when it starts to hurt.

We repeat the series of movements several times over until someone knocks at the door. Matthias wheels around. More knocking.

We haven't finished, he warns me, then goes to open the door.

At first I hope it's Maria, but disappointment takes over

when Matthias invites the visitor in. He walks into the room, leans his rifle against the wall, and puts two hares on the table. Matthias and I consult each other with a glance. Neither of us knows this man.

This is for you, the man tells us and points to the hares.

Matthias looks at the two bodies as if he were afraid they would get up and start running.

Thank you, he stammers, thank you very much. Do you want some coffee?

The visitor accepts with a nod, and when Matthias turns his back, he focuses his attention on me.

He has salt and pepper hair and a reddish beard. His face has been worn by the sun and the cold. Built close to the ground, in his fifties. Or a little older. Behind him, his rifle shines.

My name is Jean, he says. We've met before, but it was a long time ago. Back when I worked at the school with your mother.

It's true. His name awakes no memories, but his face is familiar.

Matthias serves the coffee.

I knew your father too, he goes on. Everyone knew him. I'm so sorry about what happened to him. We hadn't seen him much these last years. His garage had turned into a complete rat's nest and he stopped pumping gas. Some people said he was losing his mind, but I thought he just felt lonely.

Leaning on the counter, Matthias chooses discretion.

We were all surprised when we heard you were back, Jean says, changing his tone. I'm happy to see you're getting better. Maria told us you'll soon be on your feet.

Jean takes a big gulp of coffee and glances at his watch.

Actually, I came here to ask you for a favour. We need a mechanic.

His words startle me.

At first we thought of Joseph. He's a jack-of-all-trades. But some people can't stand him and we never know where to find

96

him or in what house he's sleeping. He won't listen to anyone. And he's not as experienced as you. Before there was your father, but now you're the only mechanic around.

My heart is pounding. I stare at Jean.

What do you want done?

We want to put tracks on a mini-bus so it can run in the snow. We almost have everything we need, the parts, the tools, the welding equipment. We set up shop in one of the storehouses in the old mine. When we turn on the generators, it's as bright as day in there. A great place to work. We need someone like you.

I clear my throat. I don't know if I'll be up to it.

We'll find you a wheelchair if that's what it takes. You'll show us how to go about it, and oversee the workers. As soon as you can stand up and take a few steps, that'll be good enough for us. I'll come and get you. What do you say?

The thought of being a mechanic again has my head spinning. I'm surprised they need me, but I accept without thinking twice.

Sitting down at the table, Matthias fidgets and tries to catch Jean's eye.

What's the mini-bus for? Are you getting ready for the expedition? Are you going to leave before spring?

Jean rubs his beard.

We're getting ready, but we're a long way from knowing when we'll be able to leave.

If I can do anything to help you, you'll let me know, Matthias offers. I've been promised a spot on the expedition, and I intend to be part of it.

Sure, but for the time being, the main thing is to keep taking care of him, Jean tells him, pointing his chin in my direction.

I have to get back to town, Matthias insists, my wife is there.

For a moment, I picture the arteries of the city, completely blocked by pile-ups of abandoned cars.

Yeah, I understand, Jean says, visibly irritated. Have you heard the latest news? he asks, wanting to change the subject.

Curious, Matthias and I wait for what will come next.

A few days ago, three people showed up in the village in the middle of the night. None of us knew them. They were starving and suffering from frostbite. We took them in and did our best for them. They told us they lived in a village on the coast. They were well organized there, but then looting started, and the situation fell apart fast. They had to escape. Their snowmobile broke down three days' walk from here. There were four of them at the beginning, but one of them froze to death. Jude assigned them a house, but he wants us to keep an eye on them. He doesn't trust them because they have an accent that's not from here.

What else did they say? Matthias asks, intrigued. Do they know what's happening elsewhere? Like in the city? Do they know if the electricity has come back anywhere?

They told us their story more than once when they showed up, but since then they haven't been too talkative.

That's normal, I put in.

Jean agrees, nodding his head.

In the meantime, he continues, in the village the supplies are starting to drop. Jude asked everyone to make an effort, and we agreed to tighten the rations. That doesn't please everyone, but that's the way it goes. And that shouldn't stop people from doing like me and setting snares.

Jean gets to his feet and slings the rifle over his shoulder. Then he tells me again to rest up and get stronger.

You should know that there are some bad cases of the flu in the village. You live up here, but be careful all the same. We're starting to run out of medicine, and that complicates things.

Jean heads for the door, and Matthias thanks him for the hares. My pleasure, Jean says. He'll bring us more when he can. Then he takes a last look in my direction. He'll come and get me once they have all the materials they need.

Don't worry, Matthias answers for me, he'll be on his feet.

Matthias rolls up his sleeves and puts the hares on the counter.

I don't know if I remember how to do this, he admits, turning them over. They are stiff with cold and rigor mortis. My father used to cook them in the lumber camps, way back when, but that was a long time ago.

I remember perfectly. My uncles used to ask me to fix the hares they caught. You have to delicately pull away the skin behind the shanks. Then you hold the back legs in one hand and pull on the fur that you've turned inside out.

While I peel potatoes, Matthias labours away, trying to pull off the skin completely, since the flesh is still frozen. Once that is done, he chops off the head with a hatchet, opens the belly, and empties the cavity. The guts smell strong. The smell of blood, and the forest after it has rained. Turning his head away, Matthias asks if I will be able to help them prepare the expedition.

We'll see, I tell him, I certainly hope so. I'm even willing to do your exercises if they'll help me recuperate faster.

I'm not talking about that. I mean the mechanic work, putting tracks on the minibus. Can you do that?

For ten years, I repaired dump trucks bigger than houses. Converting a minibus into a snowmobile, if I have the right parts, tools, and electricity, that shouldn't be a problem. I can do more than peel potatoes, you know.

Matthias cuts the hares into pieces and puts everything into a big pot with oil and vegetables.

Anyway, you don't really have the choice, he tells me suddenly. You owe us that, to me and everyone else. We saved your life. And it looks like I'm not the only one who wants to go to the city before the snow melts. So it works out perfect. I'll be able to go back to my wife. Waiting for spring makes no sense, the snow isn't going to stop falling, and at my age, you know, if a man has all the time he needs, it's because there isn't much left.

I think about that. Outside, the horizon has swallowed the sun. The sky is still clear, but the light is weakening.

As the meal cooks on the fire, we play a game of chess. Matthias wins, as usual. He is too satisfied to offer me a revenge match, and he retreats to his rocking chair with a book.

After a time I ask him what Jacques gave him in exchange for the cheese.

The question takes him by surprise. He drops his book onto his lap, then tells me Jacques let him choose whatever he wanted from the store's inventory.

What did you take?

Matthias hesitates.

A weapon.

A weapon?

Yes, to defend myself, if ever ...

You know how to use it?

Jacques showed me how.

I say nothing more and look out the window instead. In the sky, above the mountains, only a white line remains upon which the blue of night has come to rest.

A little later, when Matthias sets the dish on the table, an enticing smell fills the air. I get to my feet, leaning on my crutches, and make it to my chair without his help – or almost. I protest, but he insists on steadying me when I sit down. But that doesn't matter.

The meat is nicely browned and swims in a thick sauce. Before serving, Matthias clasps his hands and closes his eyes. This time the ceremony lasts no more than a second, and then he quickly dips the spoon into the pot.

Be careful, he warns me, these things are full of little bones.

We dig into the meal. We pull away the meat from the bones with our hands, and the sauce drips everywhere and sticks to our beards.

If you want it to be tender and the flavours to really come out, you have to cook it a long time, he tells me, his mouth full.

I laugh at him and let him know I want him to serve me some more. He leans over the pot and licks his fingers. Suddenly he freezes and lets out a strange rattle. I look up. His eyes are enormous as if he had seen a ghost. He stands up, knocking over his chair, and grabs at his throat. His eyes dart wildly around the room. His mouth opens but makes no sound. He pounds his chest with both hands. Big drops of saliva pool on his lower lip. The veins of his neck swell. I try to go to his side, leaning on my right leg and hanging onto the table. His face is turning blue. His pupils dilate and go black. I try to get his attention as I move closer. He is moving in all directions at once. I yell at him to stop. He doesn't seem to hear me. His hands open and close as if he were trying to grasp something. He hits his chest, but his movements are incoherent. I know there's a manoeuvre you're supposed to do, you have to stand behind the person and squeeze his stomach. But I'm still so weak, I'm not sure I'll be able to do it.

Stand in front of me, I tell him, panicking. Matthias, look at me! Stay put! Stop moving!

I punch him as hard as I can in the stomach. He takes the blow, bends in two, but nothing happens. When he straightens up again, I throw a second punch, harder this time. I can feel my knuckles push into his skinny stomach and reach his diaphragm.

A small bone flies from his mouth like a bullet and he falls to the floor, gasping for breath.

For the next two or three seconds, total silence. Then he starts breathing noisily, choking, vomiting, his whole body shaking.

I feel enormous relief, then realize I am standing on my own feet, pointing skyward like a rocket, for the first time. Meanwhile, at my feet, Matthias is like an old steam locomotive, labouring and coughing.

Snow crystals sketch out the slender contours of the trees. The flakes descend in straight lines, falling in tight formation, both light and heavy. The snow has climbed to the bottom of my window and is pressing against the glass. It is like water rising in a room from which there is no escape.

With my spyglass, I saw that an animal had come close to the house. Nothing very big. A fox. Maybe a lynx. Some animal come to devour the remains of the hares that Matthias threw outside yesterday evening after recuperating from his misadventure. The tracks are fresh, but soon the snow will cover them. Through the trees I can make out houses, but with all the snow they seem to be shrinking with each passing day. Settling into the earth. I spy on the village for a while. But nothing is moving. Maria is not going from house to house to look after people, Joseph is not carrying out his repairs, and no one seems to be coming to get me.

When he awoke at dawn, Matthias was back on his feet as if nothing had happened. He did his exercises, washed the dishes, and made black bread. But a shadow had fallen over his face.

We started a chess game more than an hour ago and it is still not finished. When it is his move, he evaluates every possibility at length. He reminds me of a weakened fighter who no longer trusts his instincts.

The room is quiet. The purring of the woodstove is the only sound. I question the lines in the palms of my hands, knowing very well that nothing and no one can help us predict our fate. Next to my bed, the chessboard holds its breath. Even if he is not in top shape, Matthias will end up checkmating me and winning the match. That is the only certainty I have.

Over the last few days, I have felt my body adjust to its new reality. My arms are growing stronger. My shoulders have straightened. When I remove my splints, my legs bend with greater ease. Only the wound on my left leg has not completely healed. The pain is slowly lessening, but the discomfort and numbness remain.

Still, with my crutches, I can change positions, I can lean and lift and swing my body. Like a wounded bird, I find a way to move. Not for long but long enough. Even if I sway and nearly topple, I can urinate on my own. When I am feeling strong, I execute a few round trips across the room.

We are still playing chess. Matthias says nothing. I have to stop myself from shouting: I have just checkmated him. His king is prisoner between my bishop and my knight. There is no escape.

When he realizes it, he looks up. He smiles a moment, then his face shuts down like a door being slammed. He puts away the game, sets his rocking chair by the stove, and packs snow into the kettle to melt.

I look toward the window. The sky is impatient. The barometer is pointing down. A few snowflakes float in the air, as if waiting for reinforcements before the attack.

Matthias sighs.

I've got nothing more to do here, he says. You might be getting better with each passing day, but I'm sinking lower. My wife is waiting, I know, I can feel it. She's waiting for me and I can't do anything about it, just look after you and watch the snow fall.

He takes the water off the stove, but when he lifts the kettle, one of the handles comes off and the whole thing falls to the floor in a cloud of steam. When the fog blows away, Matthias appears like a giant lighthouse above the reefs. A lighthouse, giant but no longer useful. For a moment, his face contorts and his fists clench as if he were trying to contain himself. Then he kicks the kettle as hard as he can and it goes flying noisily into the far corner of the room.

It's nothing, he tells me, even before I can react, it's nothing.

One of his thighs is soaked and still steaming. He goes out the door, pulls down his pants, and applies a snow compress to the burn. When he comes back into the porch, he asks me to help bandage his thigh.

As I grab my crutches and move to the table, he explains in great detail how to go about it.

It's all right, I tell him, I know how to wrap a bandage, I've watched you change mine often enough.

He was lucky. The burn looks superficial. The skin is red and oozing, but there is no blister, not yet. It must be sensitive, but in a couple weeks there won't even be a scar.

For lunch we eat hard-boiled eggs in silence, each in his own world. Later in the day, Matthias goes over to the other side and comes back with a toolbox. He sets it on the table next to the banged-up kettle and asks me to repair the handle that gave way. I pull the toolbox over and open it. The hinges creak softly. Inside the tools glitter. The wrenches, the hammer, the pliers, they shine like gold coins dug up from a royal tomb. He watches my reaction as if it were of the greatest importance.

You won't be able to fix a dump truck with that, he says, pointing, or modify a minibus, but it's enough to see whether you still like your trade. Maybe that's what will save us. You won't just be a cripple anymore, and I'll be able to get back to town.

I say nothing. I go about fixing the handle of the kettle, completely convinced that, whatever we do, whichever way we choose, our actions and decisions will be meaningless.

The day is bright. The sky has deepened. The wind died down.

Matthias is in the rocking chair. He has a book in his hand, but he hasn't opened it. I practice balancing on my crutches. Suddenly there is the high-pitched whir of a motor. Matthias gets up and we both move to the window. A snowmobile is climbing the slope in our direction. A minute later the door swings open and Joseph steps inside with his arms loaded down with sacks and cartons. Matthias pulls on his coat to help him bring in the rest.

I would like to help too, but with my crutches all I can do is drag myself from one place to the other.

When they come back inside with the last of the provisions, Joseph declares that there is no use clearing the roof of snow. Matthias looks at him, surprised.

It'll take me two days to shovel off all that, he explains, and I'd have to start all over anyway. I'd rather reinforce the ceiling beams, understand, the way they do in hunting camps before winter. That's the best solution.

I notice two butterfly bandages above his eyebrow. Exactly like what I have on my left leg, but smaller.

I've got to find wood for the supports. And I'll need help, Joseph says, pointing at me. You coming? It'll do you good, I'm sure.

I pull myself onto my crutches. A wave of happiness flows over me.

Go ahead, take my coat and boots, Matthias offers as he opens one of the boxes of provisions.

Joseph is quick about getting me into Matthias's clothes. Once he succeeds, he hands me my crutches and we go out.

It's the first time I have been outside since the beginning of winter. The snow is dazzling.

And with that thought, I take my first step, and the tips of my crutches sink into the snow. I fall face first in front of the door. Joseph laughs at me a second, then leans over, grabs me with both arms, and sets me on the back of his yellow snowmobile.

Hang on tight, he tells me.

The motor roars to life. And we're gone. I look behind and catch Matthias watching us move away before shutting the door. From this angle the other side of the house looks enormous compared to the porch buried in snow.

The cold air stings. It makes my eyelashes stick together and pinches my nostrils. It burns my lungs. We reach the line of the forest. It is more imposing than I imagined. We take a path that snakes between the trees. The way is completely virgin, smooth, and white. On each side, the spruce bend low with snow. When the path curves, Joseph accelerates so the snowmobile will not bog down and dig a trap for itself in the quicksand of snow. We come into a small clearing. I recognize this spot. Joseph slows down and stops the machine on a little rise where the wind has hardened the snow.

In front of us are targets nailed onto the tree trunks. We are at the shooting range at the foot of the mountain. A few kilometres from the village.

The winter silence is deafening.

Joseph pulls a bottle from his coat, takes a good hit, then hands the bottle to me.

You know, he says, turning to me, this is where our fathers

and our uncles came to tune up their rifles every year, at the end of the summer. Us kids used to follow them, remember? They parked their vehicles at the entrance, over there, and they walked here with their cases in their hands. They would open them up and fire at the targets. We weren't very old back then. But I remember the sound of the rifle shots. They never drank here. It was a rule. No need for anything artificial at the moment of truth, they used to say.

I watch birds quarrelling over a spot on the branches of a pine tree.

Your uncles were completely right, Joseph states, gazing at the forest around us, it was the right thing to leave before the snow fell. Life in the village isn't easy, you know. When those outsiders showed up, Jude insisted we go back to our watchman duties. I suppose you heard about that?

Yes, Jean told us.

Did he tell you that at first Jude refused to put them up more than one night? Even José didn't want to give them medicine. We had to convince them that they weren't criminals and that we had enough food for three more people.

We smoke a cigarette, sending thick spirals into the crystal air. The shooting range looks like a narrow lake caught in the snow's embrace.

Jude is getting hard to figure out. Maybe everyone is. The snow weighs heavily on our little lives. He's got a new project, I hear. With Jean, José, and some others, he wants to turn a minibus into a snowmobile. Do you realize? That'll never work! Even if they manage to do it, how far will they get? That kind of machine burns way too much gas. They'll empty the village supply and end up running out of gas a hundred kilometres further on. Then what'll they do? Go looking for help? When they didn't even want to help a few strangers who showed up here! They don't understand the only thing they'll find out there is frigid cold and the wind off the sea. Unless they head for the city and rob everyone they come across on the way there. I bet they're going to come looking for you to help them install the tracks. You're the only mechanic for miles around. I told them to get lost every time they brought up the subject, he mutters, lifting the bottle to his mouth.

I take a long drag off my cigarette and tell Joseph I should have done like him and become a carpenter.

Forget about it, he sighs, that wouldn't have changed anything. But you'd be better off not getting mixed up in that minibus business. Matthias should be careful too. The last few meetings have been pretty stormy. Some people want Jude to open the books. Other people want us to vote on every decision made. I'm trying to keep my distance, but events keep pulling me in. Judith died last week. She never got over the flu. There were complications. She was in terrible pain and José helped her cross over. Her family buried her not far from the village, in the snow. It was sad, what with her two small children. She got the flu, her temperature rose and it never came down. Even with the medicine. Ever since people get scared when they hear someone cough. Some of them are afraid of Maria, you know, because she has a lot of contact with the sick.

Joseph throws away his cigarette butt and hands me the bottle. With two free hands, he quickly sharpens the chainsaw.

And with all that, he shakes his head, pointing to his eyebrow, José knows I'm sleeping with Maria.

I ask him for another cigarette.

Everyone ends up knowing everything in a village, he continues, handing me his pack. He's been tailing her ever since. Maria can't take it anymore, he doesn't want to understand what's going on, and I'm discouraged. I'm suffocating here, this place is killing me.

Joseph gets up, goes to the edge of the clearing, and starts up the chainsaw.

We'll take that cedar there, he shouts over the stuttering motor.

When he leans under the skirt of the tree, the chainsaw roars and sends out a bluish cloud. The cedar falls. Joseph trims off the branches, and cuts three even sections of log. I stand up to help put them in the sled, but he shakes me off. That won't be necessary.

When he sits back down on the snowmobile, I smell the scent of fresh sawdust on his coat.

You know, he says, going back to his story and motioning me to give him the bottle, Matthias wants to leave this place. With or without anyone's help. That's no secret. And he's not the only one. But Matthias wouldn't last more than three days on the road. If the cold doesn't get him, some militia will. Whether he has a weapon or not, that won't change anything. He wants to get back with his wife, but like everybody else, he has no idea what's going on anywhere else. And with all the supplies I've brought you, he should just sit still for the next little while.

What about you? I inquire. What are you going to do?

I don't know, Joseph says, looking away, I don't know. What would you do in my shoes?

I shrug my shoulders and think of the topographical map. I came all the way here to see my father, but I showed up too late. My aunts and uncles left for their hunting camp and never came back. I'm living with a stranger who wants to leave as quickly as he can. I don't know what's keeping me here, outside of the fact that I can hardly stand up.

We empty the bottle in silence, then Joseph starts up the snowmobile, and we speed away through the woods.

By the time we pull up in front of the porch, I am frozen stiff. I can't even lift myself off the seat. Joseph picks me up in his arms and carries me inside. I slump in the rocking chair by the fire, and weakness overtakes me. As if the cold wanted to keep me in its embrace. I hope I won't get sick like the others in the village.

Matthias is still sorting supplies with great enthusiasm.

I thought you'd cut back on the provisions, he says. But there's beef, a whole duck, maple syrup, pâté, dried mushrooms, all kinds of things. There's even coffee.

I'm glad you're happy, Joseph tells him as he measures the distance between the floor and the ceiling beams.

Matthias expresses amazement when he discovers two bottles of wine.

Why all this? And why now?

Little by little, my blood warms enough to start flowing through my body. But the pins and needles are intolerable. I can barely follow what the two are saying.

Jude isn't the only one with a secret stash, Joseph points out. I wanted you to enjoy a little. Why not? But don't talk about it, it might cause trouble. Once, Jude locked Jacques up for two days.

What happened?

I wasn't there when it happened. Some people say that Jacques pointed a gun at someone who owed him some gas. Other people think it's just a plot. He was let go, but it's going to end badly if you ask me.

Matthias thanks Joseph and promises he will be discreet. But he tries to get more information about what happened with Jacques.

His whole arsenal was seized. Jude says it's too risky to have weapons circulating. That sooner or later, someone will make a wrong move.

The snowmobile ride completely exhausted me. My neck muscles droop and I lose a large part of the conversation. When I can finally lift my head, Joseph is installing the cedar planks beneath the central beams.

That won't straighten them up, he admits, driving in long nails with expert hammer blows, but it will keep them from sagging more. Now the clouds can dump their load on you, and you should be all right.

As I fight sleep, Joseph picks up his things. When he finishes he hands Matthias a key ring with a small plastic moose on it.

What's this? Matthias asks.

A present. If you're still here when the snow has melted, at least you'll have access to a car. Third house on the left before the edge of the village, you know, right next to the arena. Third house on the left, he repeats, in the garage.

What about the expedition?

I think Jude and the others are seeing to the preparations, but I don't really know how far they've gone. I'm sure you'll hear about it before I do.

When Joseph puts his hand on my shoulder to say goodbye, I jump as if he had disturbed me in the midst of a dream.

I have to go. Get some rest. Rest up and eat your fill, it's no time to give up. Your endurance is better already. I bet the next time we meet, you'll be walking.

I doubt it, I answer, thinking he is making fun of me.

Before going out the door, Joseph turns around and looks at us in disbelief. A few moments later, we hear him rev up his engine, then speed off.

Before I can make it to my bed, my head drops to my chest and I fall into a deep, gnarled sleep.

I wake up in the middle of the night with stomach pains. We ate too much. While I napped Matthias cooked the duck and put the best canned goods on the table. Artichoke hearts, smoked oysters, snails, roasted red peppers. He woke me up, we sat down at the table and devoured as much as we could. It was a change from soup and black bread.

Outside, a cold moon shines through the clouds. Its beams of light penetrate the darkest reaches of the room. On both sides of the window, shadows play. Joseph's reinforcement posts look like trees growing through the ceiling. Or magical beanstalks that have sprung up in the gaps between the floorboards.

Everything is still. Time is suspended from the night. Both are immobile. Like my legs in their splints. I try to fall asleep again, I think of life in the village, of Joseph and Maria. I think of my uncles. I wonder what they had on their table tonight, in the middle of the forest. As my eyelids slowly close, the little monster returns to gnaw on my sleep. I hear it scurrying around on the other side, gathering up all it can. I'd like to hunt it down with my slingshot and a flashlight. On crutches that would not be easy. I lean on my elbows and spot light coming from under the door that leads to the other side. I examine the moonlit room. Three cedar posts support the heavens, the table is there, the rocking chair, the sofa. The sofa. The sofa where

Matthias's blankets are carefully folded, undisturbed. The trap door to the cellar is open. What is he doing? What is he up to on the other side at this time of night? I hear him walking, stopping, starting again. I hear him turning things over, rummaging around, busying himself. That's it, I get it. I've identified the little animal that pilfers our supplies at night. I know what it is doing: preparing its departure.

The noise drops off for a time, my stomach pains subside, and slowly I find sleep again.

Very early the next morning, when I awake, Matthias is asleep on the sofa. He awakes as soon as he hears me moving around. Outside, the sky is flooded with light though the sun has yet to lift itself above the horizon. There must not be any embers left in the stove because the room has lost its heat. I wrap myself in my blankets and listen to Matthias's calm breathing. I could use a coffee.

The distant growl of an engine attracts my attention. I pick up my spyglass. In the clear, cold dawn, I spot a yellow snowmobile moving at top speed. It is following the dark line of the forest. There are two people on board. The driver holds the handles tightly and his eyes seem to be probing the distance. The person with him is wearing a red coat. She keeps glancing behind and holds onto the driver as if he is her best hope. Once they climb the slope of the hill, they turn onto a logging road and disappear. I lower my spyglass and think that without Joseph and Maria life in the village won't be the same. And mine won't be the same either.

The sun has been up for a while now, but the sky clouded up through the morning. The barometer is pointing at the ground. The air is heavy. I can see its weight. The snow has lost its lustre. In the village, smoke issues from the chimneys, climbs, levels off, then settles to the ground. As if it could not lift itself to the sky. Here and there flakes of ash fall to earth and form small black constellations against the infinite whiteness.

Once he has hung the washing above the stove, Matthias inspects the reinforcement posts. They help me move from the bed to the table without crutches, but still the poles get in the way. They cut back on Matthias's space when he brings in wood, sets the table, and does his exercises.

Are they going to hold up? he asks in a doubtful tone.

They'll hold up, I tell him. They're Joseph's work.

Matthias feeds the stove, opens the cellar door, and takes out a few items. I watch him rub his hands together, satisfied, before starting to cook. I ask him if an animal has been helping itself to our supplies.

No, he answers, I don't think so. I didn't see anything.

I heard noise during the night, I pursue.

Impossible. I didn't hear anything. Not last night or any other night.

He sets the food on the counter and closes the cellar door.

You must have been dreaming, he says sharply. Forget about it, get up, we're going to do our exercises.

I drop the subject and prepare for battle. I get to my feet, avoiding putting weight on my left leg. We begin. We stretch our arms toward the ceiling and rotate our wrists, and we breathe in. We bend our knees, keeping our spines perfectly straight, and breathe out. In the middle of the session, the church bells begin ringing. The echo returns from the distant mountains. It is the village alarm. Something has happened. I take my spyglass and look toward the village. Through the trees, nothing. The bells keep ringing. Finally they stop, and everything goes back to normal. According to Matthias someone will come and alert us if it's serious. If not, Joseph will tell us what happened.

A little later we hear the simultaneous growling of several snowmobiles. We rush to the window. There are three of them. One of them is moving through the village, the other is going past the forest, and the third is heading in our direction.

That must be Joseph, Matthias speculates, and takes the spyglass from me.

Unless it's Jean coming for me, I add.

The sound of the engine grows louder. The door opens. It's José. With him is a guy and a young woman. All three are armed. Matthias beckons them to sit down at the table, but they don't bother answering.

Over there, José says, pointing at the door to the other side.

The guy pushes open the door and disappears.

Matthias wants to know why the church bells rang.

We're looking for Maria, José answers. Have you seen her by any chance?

She hasn't been here for a while, Matthias says.

There are snowmobile tracks out front, José insists, his voice hostile, and they're recent.

Joseph stopped by a few days ago.

Was he with Maria? José questions us.

No, why?

Was he with Maria? he turns and asks me.

No. Guaranteed.

Behind him, the young woman is positioned in front of the door, holding her rifle in both hands. The guy comes back from the other side, shaking his head.

You looked everywhere? José wants to know.

Yes.

Everywhere?

Yes. Everywhere.

They're not there?

No, they're not there.

Shit, José swears. And in there, what's in there? he asks, pointing to the trap door to the cellar.

Our supplies, Matthias tells him, tension creeping into his voice. We keep our stuff there so the mice don't get at it.

José nods, then inspects the ceiling reinforcements.

Sorry to disturb you.

Matthias takes a step in his direction and asks again what this is all about.

Someone sliced off part of his ankle with an axe, he answers, motioning his companions to head for the door. We need Maria, but we can't find her. She can't be far. You two are sure you haven't seen her?

Absolutely, Matthias repeats.

José sighs, then exits with his friends as quickly as they arrived.

I wonder if you can survive an axe in your ankle. And if Maria could have saved that person the way she saved me.

Outside, the snowmobiles have left bluish furrows. The snow has started falling again, covering the tracks with a thin layer of silence.

ONE HUNDRED SIXTY-SEVEN

As I circumnavigate the table several times on my crutches, Matthias pours hot water into a bowl and rubs soap on his cheeks. His movements are slow and precise as he runs the razor over his skin. He rinses his face, wipes it, and looks at himself in the mirror. He might look a few years younger, but his features haven't changed. The skin of his neck still looks like a snow drift that has withered under the late winter rains.

As I go around the edge of the table, a drop of water hits my forehead. I stop. Another drop falls. I step back and examine the ceiling. Drops are running along a beam toward the middle of the room. They stretch, hang, then let go. One at a time, unhurried, before breaking apart on the floor. I picture the thick sheet of ice that must have formed without us knowing, right above our heads. With the heat of the stove, the snow must have compacted, hardened, and formed a thick block. Now it is preventing the roof from shedding its water normally. The posts can stand up to heavy loads, but water always ends up going where it wants to.

Matthias turns in my direction and I point to the leak. He watches it attentively, then pivots and places a metal bucket on the floor.

There, he says.

The drops tick off every second as if we were prisoners of a water clock. And our days were numbered.

By the end of the day, the bucket is overflowing and a small puddle has formed on the floor. As he kneels down to soak up the water, Matthias cries out softly as if someone had struck him. He leans heavily on his knees and does not move for several minutes. When I try to help him, he raises a hand.

It'll be all right, he says, bent double. I threw out my back but I'll be all right. Don't worry.

He insists on sponging up the rest of the water. His movements are jerky, as if his limbs had rusted. Darkness settles over the room. I stretch out my hand and reach the oil lamp, then hold it in my hands a moment.

Light it, Matthias tells me. No use waiting for a genie to appear.

I slip a match under the glass chimney and adjust the wick. When I get onto my crutches to go to the counter, Matthias moves toward me, bent like an uprooted tree. He blocks me. I tell him to let me past. And rest up while I make something to eat. He screams. No way that's going to happen. The kitchen is his space, his space alone. My space is the bed and the chair. And that's that. Even if he can't lift his eyes from the floor, he waves his arms in the air and orders me to go back and sit down, his voice both harsh and fragile. I retreat, listening to the drops of water beating on my patience with a disturbing sameness.

Matthias mutters to himself as he makes the meal. He is like an old moose, stubborn and grizzled, beating his hooves on the ground at the slightest pretext. I look at him out of the corner of my eye, convinced that this room will soon be too small for the both of us.

Even before I open my eyes, I hear the sound of dishes and the slap of soapy water.

I awake.

And am surprised to see Matthias already up, in tip-top shape, back straight. He is washing and drying the plates and pots he has piled on the counter. Amazingly, he seems to have recovered from his back problems. He is whistling a familiar tune, and he brings me a cup of coffee and toast. I quickly swallow down breakfast, then sip the coffee and watch the leaky ceiling. In the night, when the fire burned down into embers and the cold returned to haunt our dreams, I woke suddenly and noticed the water wasn't dripping. The drops had called off their parade. But as soon as we heated up the stove, they went back to their procession, just where they had left off.

With dizzying energy, Matthias shovels the entryway, brings in the wood, and kneads the dough to make black bread.

A beautiful day out there, he tells me, his words coming quickly.

Just as I decide to stand up and put my crutches to work, a snowmobile pulls up in front of the porch. Matthias hurries to open the door, and Jean walks into the room.

Today's the day, he announces. You're ready?

Matthias looks at me, two thumbs up. He tells me supper will be ready when I return.

You see, everything will work out, Jean adds.

Matthias helps me get out of my splints, then I put on his coat, snow pants, and boots. His hands are shaking more than usual.

You'll be all right, he says, wrapping a scarf around my neck, you can go now. But your crutches, you'll need your crutches.

He won't have to use them, Jean says, lifting me by the armpits.

Matthias watches us go out the door, blinking his eyes and wiping his forehead. As I go, I realize there is a vial of pills on the edge of the counter. The analgesics I used to take when the pain was unbearable. The container is empty, like a gourd whose last drop has been drunk.

ONE HUNDRED SEVENTY-FOUR

The warehouse door opens with a crash. We go inside and darkness envelopes us. Jean whistles twice. The place is cavernous and sound bounces off the sheet-metal walls. Then I hear the growl of a generator, and fluorescent tubes light up one after the other above our heads.

In front of me, five guys are staring as if they had seen a ghost. I recognize some of their faces, but time has worked on them. I have been away for a long time and we have become strangers again. One of them brings me a swivel chair and tells me he was there when they found me after the accident.

I'm glad to see you're getting better.

Yeah, I say, but it's taking time.

At least you don't have to do night watchman duties, he teases me.

And you're lucky. You've got the prettiest woman in the village looking after you, another guy points out as his friends laugh.

All right, that's enough, Jean orders them, pushing my chair among the tool boxes. Let's get to work.

The minibus is sitting on wood blocks. In the front, long metal skis have been fastened to the suspension. In the back, they have taken the wheels off and an impressive pair of tracks are waiting to be fitted on. I understand why Joseph said it would never work.

This is where we're at. Not bad, huh?

I glance at Jean, scratch my head, then lower myself out of my chair carefully. I slide under the minibus by hanging onto the tailpipe. I ask them to bring me light. I check how solid the axles are, what shape the suspension is in, and the brakes. While I'm underneath, one of the guys leans over me.

I thought you left here so you wouldn't have to be a mechanic like your father.

I turn and take a good look at him, then ask him to pass me a monkey wrench.

He does my bidding, but hands me more questions along with the tool.

Where were you all that time? Ten years is a while. What were you doing?

I tell him I was doing what I could to change my life.

Why did you come back? Because of the power being out?

No. To visit my father.

Jean kneels down to see what is happening. He motions to his pal to let me work in peace. In the yellow beam of light, his face looks harsher than usual. I wonder how this man was with young children, back before the power went off, when he was a teacher.

As I check one last detail, the smell of gas, the texture of grease, and the inky black of metal carry me far back in time. I don't know if my father would have agreed to come here. I don't think so, but I'm sure he would have used the situation to make a deal to his advantage.

When I finish they help me crawl out of there and sit back on the chair. Jean and his friends await my verdict. They stand with their arms hanging at their sides. I turn and look at the vehicle. The project is insane. It is like a ship. A ship of fools. A Noah's Ark. As if the clouds in the sky were about to open and drown everything.

I don't know why you need a machine like that.

Jean tells me it's for expeditions to replenish our supplies.

Snowmobiles are good, he goes on, but we need cargo space to transport material and people. We need a vehicle that can handle the snow.

I get it. But I bet you don't have adapters for the tracks.

Jean and his men give each other empty looks.

We'll have to drill through the hubs.

They all agree, but nothing happens. I repeat myself.

We'll have to drill through the hubs.

Jean issues orders to the men. One of them takes out a drill, another groups together the toolboxes next to us, and a third unrolls an extension cord to our worksite. I point to the guy I was talking to and tell him to come over.

Listen up. I want you to drill the holes exactly where I tell you. And delicately, without forcing the motor or busting the bit.

He nods, settles in, and begins drilling through the metal. As I keep an eye on him, I explain to Jean how we are going to go about it. He asks me for the details of every step to make sure he has understood.

Do you think we'll finish today?

Maybe. We'll see.

Glowing, Jean puts his hand on my shoulder and proudly declares I am the right man for the job.

Jean drives me home under the dark sky. We speed along as the headlights split the night. Beneath the snow, I sense the old mining site and the giant plateau created by the slag. Unlike Joseph, Jean drives the snowmobile in a jerky fashion, and I am afraid we will bog down every time we take a turn. Finally, we reach the porch. Matthias is standing in the open door. Without stopping the motor, Jean waves him to come over and get me. He moves toward us, his footing unsure in the snow.

The wind's come up, he calls, his voice barely audible over the motor. A storm's coming.

Jean nods, evasive. As soon as I slip down from the snowmobile and Matthias has steadied me with one arm, Jean hits the gas and heads down to the village.

So? Matthias asks me once we are inside.

We didn't stop once all day, I say, looking at my hands blackened with oil and dust. I'm hungry.

Is it going to work?

It should.

What's it look like?

Like a minibus, only with skis and tracks. A Snow Ark.

Matthias thinks about that for a time.

As I rub my legs, I watch the leak. We are going to have to plug it or find some way to lessen the sound of dripping water.

How are your legs?

Hard as rocks, but the pain isn't too bad. And your back?

As good as new, he tells me, but I can see the glaze of analgesics in his eyes.

Matthias serves me a plate of noodles.

Did they say when the expedition is leaving?

No. The minibus is still in the warehouse. They have to run
a few tests, inside.

Will they need you for that?

I suppose so.

So they won't be leaving right away. Was Jude with you?

No.

But Jean told you he'd save a spot for me, right?

We worked all day, I don't remember everything that was
said. You'll work it out with them.

I mop up the sauce with a piece of bread. Matthias has
nothing more to say. He contemplates the drops of water falling
from the ceiling.

The storm has been blowing for a week. The wind twists the trees and whips the falling snow. You can't tell whether it is coming from the sky or rising up from the earth.

The last few days, I have scarcely gotten out of bed. In the morning I massage my legs, do a few exercises, then lie down again. There is nothing else to do.

The roof is still leaking. We have stopped melting snow on the stove. We get the water straight from the leak. It is transparent, but has a strange taste, the flavour of the wood through which it has passed.

Matthias cooks all the time, as if he was trying to fill the void by making things to fill our stomachs. Again today he made black bread. This time he added meat and dried fruit and a good helping of fat. The mixture has been on the stove top since morning, and he feeds the fire carefully, slowly, to keep from burning his little slabs of black bread and meat.

It's not black bread, it's pemmican, that's not the same thing, he tells me.

When he finally puts his slabs of pemmican on the table, he looks particularly satisfied.

You can survive on pemmican for a long time, he says, a few mouthfuls are as good as a meal. That's what the explorers took with them when they headed up the rivers.

Outside, the storm rages and bangs against the porch. It howls in the chimney and whips the snow around. Then it knocks at the window and roars. We watch the show with calculated indifference. Suddenly we hear what sounds like a voice. Someone is calling from the other side of the door. Matthias is intrigued and opens up. Jonas is there. He comes in, shaking snow off his shoulders, and pulls the rocking chair toward the stove and sits down. He rubs his hands and holds them close to the heat. He stays there for some time, the way our ancestors did for thousands of years. Finally Jonas turns in our direction, moving his fingers with difficulty, the icicles in his beard slowly melting, his turquoise coat shiny with water. He opens his mouth to speak, but his thought seems to have deserted him, because he says nothing for a minute, hypnotized by the drops falling from the ceiling into the pail.

It's cold, he says in the end. And the snow, it's just not stopping. You did the right thing with those posts, you never know. I heard that a little further up, in the forest, there's twice as much snow. Twice as much snow, can you picture that?

Matthias raises his eyebrows, and I try to imagine my uncles' camp buried under four metres of snow.

What's that stuff? Jonas asks, pointing at the pemmican on the table.

Try some, Matthias tells him.

He picks up a piece, weighs it, then bites into it with his few remaining teeth.

It's a good storm, he goes on, his mouth full, a good storm. But we've seen storms before. There are storms every winter. That's the way it is. Life goes on. Storms don't stop anyone. The proof is that they left just as it was starting.

Who left? Matthias wastes no time asking.

Jonas stops chewing a moment.

Jude, Jean, José, and the others.

In the minibus?

Yes, in the minibus, you should have seen it, that machine, floating on top of the snow, that's what it looked like, like that boat in the Bible.

Matthias's face darkens.

Did they go to the city?

I don't know. They left, they left to look for food, gas, medicine most of all, for the sick people who can't get over the flu. I met them just before they left. We were the only ones outside because of the wind. I asked if I could go with them. To sell my empty bottles. They said yes, but next time. I insisted, I'm not afraid of blizzards. They told me they were enough as it was and that they wouldn't be gone long. I went home before I got too cold. They'll be back soon and I'll be on the next one, the next expedition.

How long ago did they leave? Matthias wants to know, caught off guard.

I don't know, Jonas says, thinking hard. It must be four or five days ago, yes, I think so. Whatever it is, we're expecting them any time now. We can't wait to see them. The village is empty without them. And ration day is coming fast.

He takes a big bite from his pemmican.

It's good, he compliments Matthias. A little hard, but good.

Matthias mutters something and pays no mind to the rest of the conversation.

Hear anything from Joseph and Maria? I probe.

Ah, pretty Maria, Jonas sighs. I knew what was going to happen, I knew it all the time, but I didn't say anything. Not to anyone. They ran away. What do you expect? That's the way it is. I knew that it wouldn't make sense trying to follow them. Joseph, he's no fool, Joseph. He wouldn't let anyone catch him. I'm no fool either. I don't look like much the way I am, I sleep in the stable, I go about my business, but I know everything that's going on. Now I'm the one taking care of the cows and feeding them. Someone has to keep company with those poor animals.

As Jonas goes on with his story, I glance at Matthias. He is staring into the void as if struck with paralysis. As if he had lost control of his fate.

You might not feel it, Jonas continues, but the days are getting longer. It's lighter in the morning. And darkness falls later. Usually, this time of year it stops being so cold for a few days at a time. Sometimes it rains instead of snowing. That's how it is, there are always mild spells in the middle of winter. Can I have more pemmican?

Yes, Matthias says, his mind elsewhere, take all you want.

Jonas stands up and slips a few slabs into his pockets.

That's for, that's for the road, he explains on his way out.

With all the snow that has piled up over the last few days, my window looks more like an arrowslit in a fortress. We are living in a bunker built for ambushes. Or an underground hiding place, with limited access to the world outside.

Dawn breaks slowly. Matthias is staring at the coffee maker, looking like he had not slept all night. His expression is serious, severe. I check out the horizon with my spyglass. I inspect the foot of the hill, toward the village. All quiet. Only three chimneys are smoking. It's winter, people hibernate.

We are far from the mild spells Jonas promised us; the landscape is frozen in silent stillness. The barometer branch is fixed in the horizontal position, the trees submit to the snow, squirrels huddle deep in the trunks. Even the leak stopped dripping for longer than usual. But then it goes back to its ways, always a bit faster than the day before. The drops seem attracted by our presence. By our smell, our heat, like the big meat-eaters that can never completely overcome their predator's instinct. In their veins they carry the ancient memory of their ancestors that methodically surrounded their prey before devouring it.

Suddenly Matthias slams his hand on the table. His coffee cup tips over and shatters on the floor.

This can't be! he cries. It's impossible!

He disappears into the other side and comes back a few

moments later, hiding something in the small of his back, underneath his shirt.

I have to go to the village.

I stare at him hard.

I have to go to the village, he repeats, uncomfortable, maybe Jude and the rest of them have come back, the way Jonas said. Maybe they're getting ready to go to the city now that they've tested the minibus. I have to tell them to save me a spot. That's the agreement, I have to have my spot on the minibus.

He pulls on his coat, grabs his snowshoes, and hurries out.

I finish my coffee as I watch him make his way through the snow. The porch suddenly seems enormous and perfectly calm. The only sound is the crackling fire and the faithful drips of water. I could use the opportunity to change my bandages, do my exercises, or trim my beard. Instead I think about the bottles of wine Joseph gave us. I let my eyes wander over the room. The thought of going back to bed occurs to me. Then my eyes fall on the door that leads to the other side.

I grab hold of my crutches, get to my feet, and move toward the door. The hinges turn without making a sound. A draft of cold, stale air hits me. I breathe deeply and cross over to the other side.

IV. WINGS

Once we have taken flight from this enclosed and lifeless place, you will marvel at the depth of the horizon. Already, we will be elsewhere. Already, we will be saved. You will follow my directions to the letter. You will fly away between earth and sky. You will fly, straight ahead, arms outstretched, you will let the air carry you.

I close the door behind me. A point of light glimmers at the end of the hallway, but darkness is dominant and the walls stretch out in dimness on both sides.

Anyone home?

No answer. The house is empty. Lifeless. Only Matthias's ghostly existence and my own haunt this place. My hands firmly on my crutches, I take a few steps forward. The humidity quickly penetrates my bones and stiffens my joints. I don't know how long I'll be able to keep this up.

The living room is on my right. Books are scattered across the floor beneath wide bookshelves. The books are like a heap of coal about to be shovelled into a furnace. A stone fireplace dominates the room from the back wall. Inside, there are charred tin cans and a few half-burned logs. A blanket partly covers the old sofa. A bottle of gin stands on the low table. Curtains are drawn over the windows. The cold has frozen everything in place. From the corner of the room, the television watches my every move and offers me the reflection of a middle-aged man moving forward painfully, leaning on two wooden sticks. The living room gives onto a dining room. Tinted blue from the snow blown against the windows, daylight filters in weakly. Further on, in the kitchen, cold air blows through the planks of a boarded-up window. Drafts carrying snow. Above the counter the cupboards are bare but for faded wax paper. In the sink, rags and oily cans. The floor tiles are covered with the broken necks of bottles and footprints from heavy, muddy boots.

I glance into the bathroom. It is dirty and unusable. I close the door before nausea gets the better of me. I go back to the main hallway and past the front door. Curious, I look out the peephole, but see nothing. Maybe it is defective. Or is the snow playing tricks on me? A reflex: I make sure the door is locked. I stop in front of the staircase leading to the second floor. The stairs are wide and heavily built. The wooden railing has been sculpted with a skill that belongs to another time. I hang onto it carefully, taking both crutches in my free hand, and climb the steps in my lurching manner. Upstairs, the three bedrooms are flooded with light. The round windows pour down brilliance on the unmade beds, the wardrobes thrown open, the chests of drawers emptied hurriedly, the clothing scattered on the floor. I move toward one of the windows.

The view is surprising. The line of the mountains seems to be drawn with unaccustomed confidence. The endless stretch of forest runs down to the clearing where the snow gauge stands. I feel as if I am the lookout on a ship and have finally grasped the dreadful magnitude of the horizon closing in on us.

Further down I can see the beginning of the village clearly. Really no more than a few buried roofs, four meagre plumes of smoke, and small trails leading from dwelling to dwelling like fragile gangways, threatened by the elements.

I could stay here forever, gazing at this desolate, magnificent landscape. But the cold is slowly taking hold of me. When I breathe out, a cloud of steam issues from my mouth as if I were smoking. I lean over with some difficulty, pick up a sweater from the floor, put it on, and rub my hands together.

Back in the hall I notice a door under the staircase. The access to the cellar, no doubt. A shiver runs down my back.

I don't want to catch cold, but I can't resist: I open the cellar door. Just to see.

All I can make out are the first few steps that disappear into a black, gaping mouth. I bend over, leaning on my crutches, and slip my head into the entrance. My pupils dilate and slowly I see into the darkness. Something is lying on the floor and blocking the way. I kneel down to inspect. A large black suitcase. It is heavy, and I have to brace myself against the doorframe to drag it into the hall and daylight.

In one of the compartments, I find a sleeping bag, a pair of boots, a yellow raincoat, and clean clothes. In another provisions of all kinds are carefully stacked. Canned food, jars of jelly, crackers, chocolate bars, dried dates. And Joseph's two bottles of wine and the slabs of pemmican.

I have discovered Matthias's secret provisions. This is where he squirrels away everything he can, discreetly, at night, like a greedy, stubborn little rodent.

I search further and come across batteries of every size, two flashlights, a detailed road map, knives of different formats, rope, and a compass. Everything a man needs for an expedition. Everything he needs to leave without warning. I even find an alarm clock in working order. It has been a while since my days were ordered by the passage of the hours. Time has become a viscous substance between sleep and wakefulness. Ten minutes after two, the alarm clock says as I slip it into my pocket.

As I put everything back in its place, I notice a pouch attached to the side of the suitcase. I open it. There is a small cardboard box inside. Bullets for the revolver. Now I know what Matthias hid under his shirt this morning.

I put the suitcase back in the cellar, close the door carefully, and hurry back to the porch to warm myself by the stove.

Heavy grey clouds weigh upon the landscape. They pass over the forest at low altitude and stroke the treetops, leaving a few flakes behind.

Matthias returned some time ago, but he has not said a word. We ate white rice with a few sardines. After the meal he collapsed onto the sofa, his eyes staring, like a dead animal. He has not moved since. Outside, the light grows weaker. Night is crouching at the edge of the woods, about to creep toward us like a wolf.

It's like the village is moving is slow motion, Matthias says, demoralized. Jude and the other guys haven't come back, and most people are just laying low and waiting. Some people say they must have had trouble with the minibus.

You think they'll come back?

Matthias sighs and takes the key ring out of his pocket, the one Joseph gave him.

I heard they left with the gas, weapons, and a good share of the supplies.

At the corner of his eyes and on his forehead, his wrinkles make him look like the sunset before a storm. I turn toward the window and see that the flakes are liquefying as soon as they hit the glass. The snow seems to want to change into rain.

Matthias toys with the keys and gazes at the little plastic moose.

They left, he says bitterly. They lied to Jonas, they won't be back. I should have suspected as much.

Darkness settles over the porch, but neither of us seems ready to make the effort to light the oil lamp. I get the feeling Matthias is doing exactly what I am: counting the falling drops of water and trying to sleep.

For the time being we've got enough supplies, he says after a while, but we'll have to figure out something else for food. There's no other choice.

I act like the words mean nothing to me and picture the suitcase he has hidden on the other side. And the alarm clock in the pocket of my coat.

It is a morning without light. A dull sun wanders on the other side of the clouds. For the first time since winter began, it is above freezing. It is raining and the landscape sops up every-thing, thickens, and sags onto itself.

Today, by hanging onto the reinforcement posts, I tried to put a little weight on my left leg. Gently, not pushing too hard. I could not take a step, not yet, but I'll manage one day soon.

The roof is leaking more. The drops run closer together and fall before the ones ahead of them finish their trajectory. Matthias has to empty the bucket on a regular basis to keep it from overflowing. Everything seems to be moving faster, but the comforting tick-tock of the alarm clock reminds me that the minutes are passing as slowly as ever.

I call over to Matthias and ask him what time it might be, according to him.

Why do you want to know? he replies, irritated, it makes no difference.

Just to know, I tell him, getting under his skin.

Then I pull the alarm clock out of my pocket.

That's all I needed, he growls, now that you can move around on your crutches the way you want, you start pawing through my stuff.

Furious, he grabs the clock from me and sets it on the table. The time is exactly eleven twenty-four.

At eleven twenty-eight, Matthias picks up the bucket and heads outside to empty it. But when he gathers the momentum to throw the water out, he slips and falls backward. I grab my crutches and go to the door. He is rolling on his side and moaning in pain. Finally he pulls himself up on all fours, stopping to rest on his knees. He lays a hand on the small of his back and leans forward to pick up the pail again. Then, carefully, he retreats back into the house.

Outside, the rain is falling and everything is covered in a layer of ice. The front entrance is perilous, the snow glitters, and tree branches bend and sparkle.

Get out of the way, Matthias orders me, his face twisted in pain, let me get by.

I close the door and turn around. He hurls the bucket at the wall.

They left for the city! Do you get it? Where else would they have gone? They took everything they could and left me behind. That's what happened – that and nothing else!

He is struggling like a bear caught in a trap. I try to make it back to my bed without riling him up. I stretch out and avoid moving, lying low.

They don't give a shit about me! he bellows, kicking the pail that rolled back in his direction. And I didn't see it coming. You understand? A man my age! A bunch of pissants, all of you! You can't understand. You have no respect for anything. I want to see my wife again! Is that so hard to understand? My days are numbered. I prayed, but everything is behind me now. I want to be with her, I want to be at her side. That's all that matters. I don't care about the rest.

The clock says four fifty. Despite all of Matthias's carrying on, I fell asleep. I move my legs and sit up in bed. The battered bucket is under the table, and the leak is falling directly onto the floor. A little river crosses the room, heading for the sea.

Matthias is sleeping on a chair, mouth open, head thrown back. It looks as though his heart has simply stopped. On the table before him, his key ring, a book, and a bottle of wine. Empty.

It is still raining, and everything lies beneath a thick layer of ice. A few trees have fallen to the ground. Others have lost big branches. The electric poles are scattered across the snowy fields, laid low by the weight of their wires. The ice storm has fossilized the landscape in crystal glass. Even the snow gauge has been petrified.

When I stretch out my arm to take my crutches, Matthias springs to life, as if someone had slapped him in the face.

Where do you think you're going? he growls, his teeth stained with wine and his speech slurred. Look outside, go and take a look, he insists, pointing toward the window. Where do you think you're going to go? There's nowhere to go. We've been left behind. Look, go ahead! Look as much as you want! There's nothing to see. We're caught in a trap in a sea of ice. Twenty thousand leagues under the snow.

His glassy eyes glitter briefly, then flare out. He grabs the bottle by the neck and sucks out the last drops.

We'll never get out of here, he declares, banging the bottle back onto the table. Winter won't give us a second chance.

He belches and adjusts his position to look at the clock. Three minutes after five.

All that happened over two centuries ago, he tells me, pointing at the book in front of him, in a magnificent and God-fearing city, celebrated for its churches, basilicas, and cathedrals. It was a quiet morning, even the waves entered the port on tiptoe. The entire population had gathered to attend Mass. Suddenly, the water drew back from the shoreline. The birds rose into the sky. The dogs began to bark, seeking out their masters. And the earth shook. Crevasses opened up in stone walls, the mortar between the bricks split apart, and clouds of dust tumbled to the ground. The sculpted arches, the pinnacles of the belfries, the painted domes – nothing resisted. The vaulted ceilings collapsed on the praying people. Buried alive in the churches. And when they rushed into the street to gaze upon the damage, Matthias declares with a glance at the crucifix above the door, the survivors were swept away by a tidal wave.

Darkness is slowly swallowing the surroundings. A snake digesting its prey. Matthias picks up the oil lamp, his head nodding. Several matches break between his fingers before he manages to light a flame inside the narrow glass chimney. I listen to the seconds turning circles inside the clock as if they were trying to stall for time.

What the hell are we doing here? he shouts, waving his hands in the air. We're caught in a trap. We're stuck. We're screwed. Look at the clock, watch how the hands move, listen to the sound it makes. It's not cold or snow, it's not darkness or hunger. It's time – time will destroy us. It's five seventeen, and no prayer will get us out of this place. Are you listening?

Matthias gets to his feet and points his finger at me. Then he staggers and sits down again.

We don't have a prayer, he repeats, his voice hoarse.

It is five twenty. Matthias has calmed down. His eyelids droop as if he were hypnotized by the silence that separates each second.

Maybe you should lie down on the sofa, I suggest gently.

His eyes pop open like a glowing forge made red-hot by the bellows.

Are you telling me what to do? Are you my mother or something? You're the one making decisions and issuing orders? You're still limping, but your wounds have healed. You don't need me anymore, is that it? My presence is an annoyance, I disturb you, and you're trying to tell me so? Oh, you're doing better, but what are you going to do next? Do you have somewhere to go? Or do you want to stay here? The snow is piling up, the food is running out, and people are deserting the village. I can't believe I'm still stuck here, he spits between clenched teeth, it makes no sense.

His eyes narrow as he looks at me, a target in his crosshairs.

It's your fault. This is all your fault!

He picks up the alarm clock and throws it at me as hard as he can. I barely have time to duck as it shatters into pieces against the window frame. I look up and see the wine bottle coming my way, end over end, smashing just above my head. He gets up, turning over his chair in the process, moves around the table, and comes lurching in my direction. I want to move and react, but I am paralyzed. Matthias stands over me like a thundercloud. I hear the air rush into his lungs, rattle around his chest, and exit through his nostrils. He grabs my chin and forces me to look him in the eye. I feel his fingers squeezing my jaw and crushing my cheeks. This old man with the black, hard, bulging eyes is a stranger. I don't know what he wants or what he is going to do.

Joseph is gone, he can't defend you now, he says, slurring his words. Nobody will help anybody anymore. You understand? You're doing better. You're talking and you can move around. But nothing has changed here. I'm the one who makes the decisions. You got that? Here, you do what I tell you to. Answer me – you got that?

Saliva sprays my face as his bony hand holds me prisoner. I reach out to grab one of my crutches, but he reads my mind. With one hand he pushes them out of reach. With the other he steps up the pressure, pushing my head deep into the mattress.

Look at me, he thunders. I'm twice your age. But I won't be pushed around. Not by you. Not by Jude. Not by anybody in this place!

Our breath comes hard and fast. Our eyes are glued to each other. Then, for a split second, I sense a weakness in the muscles of his face.

Everything happens very fast. I let out a shout. Matthias is startled. I push him away and free myself from his grip. I slip off the bed and crawl toward the door, paying no attention to the shards of glass on the floor. Matthias grabs my ankle. I fight back with my other leg. Though the pain blinds me, I manage to kick him in the crotch. I knock the wind out of him, and his balance goes. He falls backward, hitting a post and knocking it flat as he falls.

When he gets to his feet among the upended chairs, his nostrils flare and he is staring straight ahead. He sizes me up, picks up one of my crutches, and waves it in the air like a club. I dodge the first blow by backing against the wall. I parry the second with the stool that stands by the front door. I ward off his assault and look for a way out. If I manage to stand, he'll knock me down. If I open the door to escape, I won't get further than a few metres. I throw the stool, but I don't have much strength, and it falls to the floor before reaching its target. Matthias attacks again, I roll in a ball to protect myself, the crutch slams into one of the posts that breaks free from the impact. He roars in pain; the blow must have travelled up his hands.

He prepares to attack again as I try to reach the poker from the stove. Suddenly, a groaning sound startles us both. Matthias freezes on the spot, but I stay in my defensive crouch, keeping my eyes on him. I hear water pouring onto the floor. He has recovered his senses and stares in amazement at the state the room is in. I lift my head and glance at the ceiling. There are four or five leaks now. And the window next to my bed is cracked from one end to the other.

A great boom shakes the porch. Seconds later, the window explodes into pieces, icicles fall away from the roof, and cold air invades the room.

Matthias stands there, uncomprehending, like a monument from a bygone age. Outside, the rain has changed back into snow and the wind rushes in to scatter flakes on the floor, the bed, and the stove. The beams groan dangerously. Matthias looks at me. Winter is walking on our heads. Then part of the ceiling collapses and knocks him to the floor under a tonne of wreckage, pieces of sheet metal, and blocks of ice.

V. MAZE

You will fly, straight ahead, arms outstretched.
Let the air carry you. I will keep an eye on you
as I gain altitude. Discreetly, without attracting
your attention. Like a member of the team breaking the rules, I will surrender to the headiness
of flight. High above, everything will be clearer,
more beautiful, and finally I will give myself over
to the light.

The porch is a heap of snowy debris, and a wide expanse of sky stretches above our heads. The lamp was spared by the collapse, but it fell off the table and shattered, and the pool of oil continues to burn. I pick myself up and hurry to throw snow on the flames. The room goes very dark with only the light of the night sky coming through the breach in the ceiling. I turn my attention to Matthias. He is unconscious but still breathing, I believe. His legs are buried beneath a broken beam, twisted sheet metal, and snow. I try to free him by pulling on his arms, but it is no use. I kneel by his side and dig at the snow with my hands. I push aside the blocks of ice, pull away the sheet metal, and with a piece of wood prevent the beam from collapsing further and crushing his legs. Despite the numbing cold, I manage to grab him by the armpits and pull him across the floor. He is heavy. Like the dead weight of a corpse I must hide. I pause for a moment and lift my eyes toward the snowy sky. We were lucky after all: part of the roof still holds.

Everything could have ended here, I say, shivering. Everything could have ended. But it didn't.

I go back to work, take hold of Matthias again, and carry him over to the other side.

I set him on the sofa in the living room and cover him with blankets I found upstairs. I consider tying his hands, but decide not to. I picture the scene over and over, and I don't understand. The man who was boiling with anger a few minutes ago is now pale and fragile.

There is no wood in the room. To light a fire in the fireplace, I break two chairs into pieces. But the wood burns fast and the heat disappears up the large stone chimney.

For a time I try to sleep by curling up on the love seat, but I'm cold and my legs hurt too much. I get up, smash another chair, and sit in front of the fireplace, massaging my painful limbs.

The night deepens as I stare at the room in the wavering firelight. The bookshelves, half empty, the open drawers of the furniture, the shards of dishes, the disorder, it all reminds me of pictures of earthquakes or tidal waves.

I go to the window and open the drapes. A greyish glow is dispersing the night and refracting on the built-up frost. From here I have more or less the same view as from the porch. With the forest, the clearing, and the snow gauge. All that is missing is the wood barometer. Tirelessly, a few flakes try to appease the appetite of the earth, but they are swept aside by the wind. The landscape tilts, fossilized in ice. Even the great spruce trees are downcast. Further on I can imagine the high-tension lines embracing the ground as a sign of their obedience.

Matthias has not moved. I check his pulse. It seems normal. I don't know if he is sleeping or unconscious. I examine his legs. A few scrapes, some contusions, but no more. He was lucky: the beam could have crushed his tibias.

When the sun has given the clouds a lighter hue, I make a trip to the porch to gather up a few necessary items before the snow takes possession of everything. As I open the door, I consider what remains of the roof's unstable structure. A few beams holding up tons of snow. Dislocated sheets of metal. Planks split from one end to the other. Twisted nails. After I have evaluated it all, I take a deep breath and venture into this shipwreck about to sink at any moment.

The first thing I notice as I skirt the heap of ice and debris in the middle of the room is one of my crutches, the one Matthias damaged by smashing it against a post. I waste no time: I empty the drawers and take what was on the counter. I unhook the saw, the pots and pans, and carry my booty to the other side, limping all the way.

I return and start pushing aside the snow, the blocks of ice, and the rest of the wreckage. I need more time, not to mention a shovel. Still I manage to unearth some canned goods, one of my splints, the axe, and Matthias's snowshoes. Very little, really. Avalanches sweep away everything in their path.

On my knees, on the floor, I have to face the facts. There's no sense digging deeper. The porch is a collapsed roof with a dangerous heap of snow balanced on it. A fortress conquered by the enemy.

A patch of blue sky glimmers above my head, through the breach in the roof. The ceiling beams begin to groan. It is time to go back to the other side. When I close the door, the walls vibrate, and the remaining section of roof collapses in a final racket. I try to open the door, I push on it, I throw my shoulder against it, but it refuses to budge.

That's the end, I realize, the rest of our things are buried under ice and snow. Our provisions, the stove wood, my map – everything.

When I return to the living room to tally up what we have left, our supplies, Matthias is staring straight ahead.

What was that noise? What's going on? Where are we? Where's my wife? How is she doing?

Shut up! I tell him. Completely discouraged.

We've been on the other side for a few days now. The Arctic cold has returned. The days are dazzling and the nights are endless. Matthias and I each sleep a few hours at a time to keep the fire going. The fireplace must have been purely decorative. If we let the embers die, it will take a whole day before the room is warm again.

Matthias has recovered incredibly quickly. As if nothing had happened at all. A little scrape on his forehead, a few scratches on his legs, that's it. He has not brought up what happened on the porch. Maybe he is ashamed. Or maybe he just doesn't care. He has started telling me about a book he just finished in which a man lost in a dark forest finds the door that leads to hell.

I listen to him and figure I would be better off on my own. Finding a place to live in the village. But I doubt I would be able to. Like convicts on a chain gang, he and I must resign ourselves to our fate.

And so we do: today we fixed up the salon, broke down several pieces of furniture, then sorted our precious supplies. We moved the television out of the room because of the screen's reflection. In the evening, it multiplied the candlelight and the glow from the fireplace, and that was good. But during the day, it broadcast our image. Our emaciated faces, our greasy hair, our messy beards, and our dirty, torn clothing.

We take a break and share a can of creamed corn. Matthias offers to go to the village this afternoon to see whether he can't get his hands on some food.

The minute he's gone, I promise myself, I'm going to search his secret reserves on the cellar stairs. The very minute he leaves.

You say something? he asks, making sure there is nothing left in the can.

No, why?

Just wondering.

Later, when I am dozing off and resting my leg, I think I hear the little rodent again. It is slipping along the walls, sneaking through the doorways, making sure its supplies are where they are supposed to be.

I wake up with a start. Matthias is gone. I look out the window. A pitiless snowstorm has wiped out the landscape. I spot a slow shadow making its way toward the village, pulling a suitcase.

I knew it.

The suitcase is gone from the landing of the basement stairs. I stand in front of the stairway that disappears into the emptiness. For a moment I remember the character in Matthias's book, and begin my slow descent into the realm of shadows. Maybe I will find something that escaped the rodent's attention.

With all the effort I've made over the last few days, my left leg could give out at any time. Yes, I can walk now, but I am still weak and need a new pair of crutches, or a cane, something to lean on.

With one hand I feel my way the best I can, using the wall, and in the other hand I hold a candle whose light blinds me even as it illuminates the stairs. The way down is steep, and the steps protest each time I move forward. The supports could give way without warning. When I finally reach the bottom, I smell the fetid breath of the damp earth floor.

I explore the cellar, bent double to keep from banging my head on the support beams and the shiny copper of the pipes. No one seems to have been down here since the power went out. But that can't be true – I bet Matthias knows this spot like the back of his hand. And others have been through here before him.

The furnace sits like a deposed king in the centre of the basement. It is sleeping deeply. Its eyes are closed beneath its mask of soot and iron. I would have to wake it up if I wanted to heat the house. But there is nothing to feed it and bring it back to life. Birchbark is scattered across the floor next to a small pile of kindling. That's the extent of it.

I turn to look behind me and spot a workbench where tools are resting among screws, nails, and bolts. Attached to the wall are tall shelves with bins, tires, rope, and fishing tackle boxes. A pair of snowshoes and ski poles catch my eye.

That's it, I tell myself, satisfied at last, I found what I need.

I inspect the cellar systematically now, peering into every corner, opening boxes, taking my time. Under the stairs I come upon a chainsaw, a gas can, nearly empty, and a quart of oil. I discover the power box on the wall. I open it and flip the switches, an absurd act of hope. Nothing happens. My candle is burning down to the end, and I put it out before it scorches my fingers. The underground darkness closes over me. Little by little my eyes grow accustomed to it, and I can make out the blue glow filtering down from the stairway. I lean heavily on my ski poles, but I am afraid my foot will slip and get stuck between two steps. Either that or a monster will grab me by the ankles and drag me into the darkness to be devoured.

When I look up, I see a shadow at the top of the stairs. It's Matthias.

I am amazed he's back. I did not hear him return, and to tell the truth, I was hoping he was gone for good.

He takes my snowshoes and poles and helps me climb the last steps.

It's dark down there, isn't it?

You said it, I agree, and go into the living room.

The ice storm finished off the village, he reports. Trees and lamp posts are lying everywhere, in the middle of the street. Some of the houses are completely encased in ice. Petrified, turned to stone. I didn't see anyone. I knocked on doors when I saw smoke coming from the chimney. They let me in. The people in the house, their faces were grey and drawn. But they were nice enough. They asked me who I was. I told them my story, and they gave me three partridges they'd caught that day. Food is getting more scarce, they warned me. The little that was left was eaten in less than two weeks, and they had to look everywhere for provisions. And go hunting. They said another group left the village just before the ice storm. They wanted to take advantage of the thaw to reach the coast. They said power had been re-established in that sector. And that people were able to harness wind turbine energy. There were a dozen or more of them, on snowshoes, on skis, with children, food, and equipment on sleds. Jacques went with them, or so they said. I didn't even know he was still around.

As I listen to his story, I pick up one of the partridges. It is plump with reddish feathers. I put my feet on its wings and pull on its legs. The plumage stays on the floor and the breast, in one piece, ends up in my hand. I throw a cupboard door in the fireplace and cut the flesh into thin slices. When the embers are nice and red, I fry the meat in a pan that I put directly on the flames.

Matthias watches me and salivates.

After we eat, he stretches out on the sofa and stares vaguely at the ceiling fixture.

Where's the black suitcase that was on the landing, on the basement stairs?

Slowly, Matthias pivots his head in my direction.

Your backup supplies, I continue, where are they?

I don't know what you're talking about, he stammers. Our supplies are buried in the cellar beneath the porch under a tonne of debris.

I saw the suitcase on the basement landing, it was black, I saw it and it's not there anymore.

Maybe, but we just ate partridge and it was delicious. You should lie down and sleep a little, it'll do you good.

I curse and throw a few pieces of chair rungs onto the fire. The room appears and disappears in the dance of flame and shadow.

We still have some food left. And two partridges. We're good for another few days, Matthias tells me. We lost a lot of things in the porch, but soon we'll find a way out. Don't worry. Sleep, he advises, I'll look after the fire.

I curl up in a ball, as far as possible from him and as near to the fire as I can be. Like a stray dog that has stopped trusting anyone. I think of my aunts and uncles again. I picture them laughing at the monstrosity of winter, and I figure a stubborn mind can conquer anything. I lost the map Joseph gave me, but I remember the "x" of their hunting camp by the river. And I remember the legend too, at the bottom of the map, that showed I am only a miniscule dot compared to the crushing power of the forest.

It has been snowing for five days straight. The ice storm is a distant memory, buried like a layer of sedimentary rock in a cliff face.

To keep warm we have burned most of the furniture in the house along with the shelves, the stair railings, and the doors to the rooms.

Our food supply is at its end. All our meals are the same, but Matthias eats whatever I put in front of him without any comments. He has refused to go back to cooking. Several times I question him about his secret provisions. Every time he denies, refutes my allegations, and ridicules me.

Yesterday, finally, my stubborn questioning angered him. He threw his book on the floor, picked up one of my ski poles, and threatened me, shouting. His eyes were hard and glittering like a vein of quartz. Fear turned my bones to liquid, but I stared at him and would not react. He took a deep breath, calmed down, and went back to his chair. A few moments later he was smiling; once again, he had succeeded in avoiding the question.

Day's end settles over the landscape. The mountains turn purple with evening light. These are the first rays of sunshine we have seen in a long while. But night extinguishes them in no time.

Matthias is reading by candlelight. From time to time he

glances down and plays with the hot wax, then goes back to his book. The flame lights his face from below, and the shadow of his nose joins the one cast by his eyebrows to draw a wide black stroke across his forehead. He looks like he is wearing a mask.

Later, as I am peeling potatoes, he sits next to me and begins playing pensively with the plastic moose that decorates his key ring.

I have a story for you, he announces, I just read it, so listen. A long time ago there lived a humble peasant. He was hard-working, but his fields were as poor as he was. One autumn, to his great surprise, his land bore fruit the way he could never have imagined. From that year on, his harvests were more abundant than the year before. But since he could not explain the miracle, he said nothing to anyone. He built an enormous barn and stored as much as he could. When it was full to the brim, he built another, bigger than the first. Destiny had smiled upon him, and he thanked his lucky stars. No misfortune could strike him. His future was assured: he would simply eat, drink, and rest. One day a neighbour came to visit to borrow a sickle, for his was broken and the fate of his family depended on his harvest. But he could not find the peasant anywhere, neither in the fields nor in the house. Worried, he searched the farm. When he saw the enormous, overflowing barns, he was astonished. And stupefied when he came across the peasant's body on the ground. As if his soul had suddenly been taken from him, without warning, as he was strolling peacefully on his property.

I take the potatoes out of the water. We let them cool down, watching the steam lift into the air.

You see, Matthias says, that's why I'm not hiding anything. If I had reserves, I'd share them with you.

I lift my eyebrows.

We need food, as well as candles and an oil lamp, he states. We need a lot more things, but we have to start with the essentials.

I don't answer. I wonder what he has done with his revolver.

Perhaps it is buried under the porch roof. Or concealed in a suitcase full of supplies. Unless it is still in his belt.

Tomorrow I'm going to the village, he continues, to ask if someone can help us out. If that doesn't work, I'll search the abandoned houses. There have to be some provisions somewhere.

I look up at him.

I'm going with you.

There's no chance of that, he replies sharply. Tomorrow I'm going to the village and I'm going alone. You'd only slow me down. And if people see that you're on your feet, they'll say that we can get along on our own, and they won't give us anything.

I'll help you search the empty houses.

Look at your legs, he insists, you're getting stronger, but you still don't have the endurance. You limp like an old man. And what about me? I'd never have the strength to drag you the rest of the way if you give out halfway back. In a few weeks, maybe you'll be up to it, but for now, forget about it.

We'll see, I tell him.

That's it, we'll see, he repeats, exasperated.

This morning, when I awake, Matthias is gone, the fire has died, and the room is cold. Just my breathing and the heavy beating of my heart. I dress quickly and rush up the stairs, as if my legs had never known pain.

By moving from one window to the next, I get a good view of the surroundings. The snow gauge is still visible in the clearing, buried up to its neck. Further on the forest carries its burden of ice. At the bottom of the hill, three tenuous plumes of smoke reach toward the clouds. Matthias's footprints go down to the village like a dotted line.

I take a moment to think. The village is both very close and very far. I know I'm doing better, I can feel it. But what if Matthias is right? Maybe I would never make it to the village. Maybe I'm still too weak. And too impatient.

I lift the window and stick my head outside. The air feels good, and the cold envelopes my body languorously before slipping into the house. I take a deep breath and lay my hand on my left leg.

Now's the time, I tell myself, to go see what Matthias is up to. I'm going down to the village.

I hurry down the stairs awkwardly, dress warmly, take my ski poles and snowshoes, and open the door.

Immediately, the snow blinds me. The snow's sombre light.

If I fall I will never get up again. If I fall I will disappear beneath the surface. Thousands of years from now, people will find the remains of an anonymous ancestor mysteriously preserved in ice.

I get a hold of myself, tighten my hands around my poles, and take a few steps. Just like that, I recover the feeling of freedom I thought I had lost forever, under my car, among the twisted metal and shards of glass.

The way down to the village is longer than I thought, but everything goes according to plan. I follow the path Matthias made. Each step is calculated, and I hold firmly onto my poles.

All is quiet. Normally with the cold you would hear the metallic chirping of the power lines, as if hundreds of birds were flying back and forth down a narrow conduit. But today, I hear only my snowshoes tamping down the snow and the lamentation of the wind in the cables hanging here and there. Some of them are so low I could grab one just by lifting my arm – with no fear of being electrocuted by the current.

I reach the edge of the village. The first houses stand to my right, buried in snow, mute. I stop and look. I have never seen so much snow, I can scarcely believe it. I walk past rooflines, dormer windows, chimneys. Normally there would be enormous piles of snow on either side of the street, and I would move between the white walls as if I were in a trench.

The main street stretches straight ahead, but I have to move around the tree branches and fallen lamp posts that block the way. Some houses are difficult to spot because of the snow heaped high around them. Further on I recognize my father's garage. The sign advertising the price of gas emerges from the snow like the hand of drowning man from the waves. I think of the world buried beneath my feet. I wonder what drove me to come back here. And why I could not leave the past to fade away by itself, in the arcana of my memory. I wanted to see my father again, I wanted to change the way things had been, and I failed on both accounts. My father died before I could reach him, and whatever I do, whatever happens, I will always be a mechanic, as he was. The important choices in my life were made a long time ago, and I have to live with them.

I continue following Matthias's tracks. They lead to a small network of paths that run from one house to the next. The village is frozen solid, and only three chimneys have smoke coming from them.

In front of me, at the end of the street, I spot a figure. I don't think it is Matthias, but I want to be sure. I wish I had brought my spyglass. The person disappears down a side street. Whoever it is has not seen me. Unless they are pretending not to.

Further on I recognize the house that lost its roof in the fire. The charred rafters stand out against the whiteness of the snow, and the ice has given them a striking lustre, black and luminous. As if winter were toying with a burned skeleton that did not receive proper burial.

I cross the bridge to the centre of the village. A ray of sun shines through, and for a moment the air seems milder. Near the town hall, in the golden light, a man is leaning against a tree. I squint. It's Jonas. I recognize his turquoise coat. I move toward him. My leg is giving me serious pain. I'm going to need to take a rest. When I reach him, Jonas gives me a mocking look.

I saw you coming, he says, chewing on something. You walk so slow, you give everyone time, everyone time, to see you coming.

What are you eating? I ask, sitting down in the snow.

Pemmican, he tells me, and proudly displays the piece he is holding in his hand. Matthias gave it to me. It's good, really good pemmican. There's not much meat left in the village. No one can go hunting. There are no guns anywhere. We looked everywhere. Jude and the others took them all. No one knows when they're coming back. But I don't want anyone to kill any more cows. I'm the one who takes care of them. I feed them, I clean the stalls, and they keep the stable warm. I sleep real good in the hay.

Where did he go?

Who?

Matthias, I say, trying to catch his eye, Matthias.

He came from that way. We talked. He promised me he'd give me more pemmican if I helped him find some gas. I told him I'd see what I can do. It's easy, there's some at Jude's place. Eight canisters and I'm the only one who knows where they are. That's going to be a lot of pemmican.

Where did he go?

I don't know, I think he went toward the arena. But watch out, don't go, don't get too close to the arena. The snow, the roof collapsed, and parts of the wall are falling, piece by piece, and they don't warn you first.

Jonas leans over and stares at me, scratching his head.

You're going to catch cold sitting on the ground, he warns me.

He helps me to my feet and hands me my ski poles.

Anyway, winter, winter is coming to an end. The river has started to break up. You don't see it, but you can hear it. If you know how to listen.

For a time we say nothing. Total silence.

It's getting humid. Last night there was a halo around the moon. It's going to snow pretty soon. A snowstorm, just one more, then it's going to start melting. And after, after the snow, when the roads are clear, I'm going to be able to sell my bottles.

Where? I ask him, smiling.

On the coast somewhere, in a grocery store.

Jonas's face shines, then a shadow falls over him.

I have a lot of bottles. And they're heavy. I'll need a car. And I don't know, I don't know how to drive. And I don't have a licence. Matthias promised, he promised to take me there if I find him some gas. Do you think I can trust him?

I clear my throat.

I'm sure, I say, looking at the church a little further on, that he's a man of his word.

Jonas's face lights up again. He smiles at me, slips his pemmican back into his pocket, and moves off.

I evaluate the condition of my left leg. The rest did me good. The pain is stable. I can keep on.

As I head for the arena, the clouds knit together above the village and the landscape turns dull. In front of the church, I notice snowshoe tracks. I look up. One of the doors is ajar. I go to the entrance. Without a sound, I ease my head through the doorway.

It's dark inside, but the grey light of day passes through the dull stained-glass windows. On one of the pews, close to the altar, I recognize Matthias, his bent shoulders. He is on his knees. I believe he is praying.

I retreat and walk quickly away from the church. I hide behind the rectory. This way, he won't be able to see me. And I will be able to follow his next move.

It is not very cold, but since I am not moving, my limbs and the muscles of my face have gone numb. I start sneezing. Every time I do, I am afraid Matthias will step out of the church and see me. The door finally opens, and Matthias comes out. He looks around, then follows the path. I let him get ahead of me, counting to ten, then start to tail him. I hide behind trees that have fallen under the weight of the ice, telephone poles, and the corners of houses. I suspect he isn't the kind of man who keeps looking back, but you never know.

Despite his age he moves quickly, and I have to work to keep up. I lose sight of him near the arena. I stop and wait and look at the building, a prisoner of the snow. It has become a heap of twisted metal buried beneath an avalanche of silence. Like the porch, but on a bigger scale. Not a shipwrecked vessel, but a great steamship that has struck an iceberg.

Snow begins to fall. The flakes are delicate, as if they have been ground to powder inside the clouds.

I continue to trail Matthias. As I go past the arena, I spot him entering a house. I stop and wait. It is the third house on the left, before the edge of the village. The house with the garage. The one where Joseph grew up. Like the others it seems to have been abandoned, and some time ago. I move forward carefully, leaving tracks in the soft snow, and suddenly I feel very far from the living room and the fireplace. If I go in and Matthias sees me, he will fly into a rage, and I do not have the strength to calm him down. Or run for my life. I circle the house, peering into the windows, but it is dark inside, and I can't tell if he is there. I retrace my steps and notice a small pane of glass on one side of the garage. Snow covers part of it and I have to kneel down to look in.

I look, but don't see much. Matthias is behind a car. He opens the trunk and leans in. He rummages through a large black suitcase. A shiver runs through me. He is sorting pemmican, canned goods, boxes of cookies. He is taking notes on a scrap of paper and counting on his fingers. When he finishes he gets in behind the wheel, takes out his key ring, and stares at the plastic moose hanging from it. He starts the engine and lets it idle for a while. His eyes shine, as if one of his wishes were about to come true. Then he cuts the motor, sets a photo on the dashboard, and begins to pray.

I sigh. It is all so predictable. I did not need to come this far to understand. Matthias is preparing his departure. I won't be able to stop him. I am jealous – it is that simple.

When I stand up again, I can hardly feel my leg. I rub it, exercise it, but to no effect. When I tighten the straps on my snowshoes, I feel like I am leaning on a phantom limb, but after a few minutes of walking, the feeling returns little by little. And with it the pain.

The tracks I have left are visible for all to see. I can only hope the falling snow will conceal them from Matthias.

I move past the arena again, then the church. I cross the bridge and trudge down the main street. My leg is hurting. A sudden wave of fatigue overtakes me. I will need to rest before making the climb back to the house. Rest and warm up.

I choose one of the paths that leads toward a house that seems inhabited, even if no smoke is rising from the chimney. As I draw near, the snow weighing upon the roof makes my head spin. I take off my hat and scarf so my face is visible, and I knock on the door and wait. On the porch are several cords of wood, tall and tightly stacked. I knock harder. No answer. I open the door.

Hello?

No one home.

I pull off my snowshoes and move into the snowy shadows of the house.

There are boot tracks on the floor. Dirty dishes on the counter. Empty cans. I look in the cupboards: rice and flour. A good stock of potatoes, canned meat, and instant coffee. Dazzled by this wealth of supplies, I take a little of each and put everything in a bag. That way, nothing will be too obvious, and I will not go back empty-handed.

I go into the living room and put my hand on the woodstove. The metal is warm. Someone made a fire today. I sit down on one of the armchairs and set the bag on my knees. I unbutton my coat and exhale. My leg is hurting and my heartbeat is located next to my knee.

A heap of blankets lies near the stairway. The floor is covered by a large rug, a few items of clothing, and gossip magazines. My eyelids grow heavy. I fight sleep at first, shake myself, remind myself I have a long walk back. Then I drift off, momentarily forgetting the shooting pain in my leg.

Suddenly I'm awake. I heard someone cough. I'm sure I did. It wasn't a dream. I turn around. I feel someone watching me. No one. No sound in this room.

It is still light out, but I don't know how long I might have slept. I take my bag, get up, and walk toward the door. As I button my coat, I hear something again. Like the rattle in someone's chest. It's coming from upstairs.

I will go and see.

The stairs creak under my weight.

On the second floor, a hall and three bedrooms. The doors are open. I look into the first room. Two people are in bed and a third is lying on pillows on the floor. They are not moving, but I hear them breathing. They are thin and pale. Their faces are hollow and their eyes so sunken I can see the bones of their skulls. I take a step, then hear a voice from the room next door. It is so weak and wavering I can hardly understand it.

Jannick? Is that you, Jannick?

I don't answer. I go back down the stairs, making no noise, then out the door, leaving the bag of food on the front porch. They need it more than we do.

I cross the deserted village on my snowshoes. The wind has picked up. My tracks fade in the blowing snow, but still, they are visible. Matthias could follow me step by step if he wanted to.

I adjust my scarf and trudge toward the edge of the village. The snow is dense and the crystals slash through the air sideways as if they were cut from sheet metal. I am limping seriously now. I have trouble lifting my left foot, and my snowshoe drags in the snow. I understand why neither my uncles, nor Joseph, nor Jude wanted to take me with them. I am not strong enough. Nor agile. The first obstacle would have killed me and they wouldn't have been able to do anything about it.

The sky has become a grey glow behind whirlpools of snow. I look up and try to situate myself in this empty landscape. Around me everything is black. Around me everything is white. To one side I can make out the dark line of the forest. It is the only sign that I am not moving through a desert.

I begin the climb toward the house. The slope is steeper than I thought. My breathing is laboured. My leg is numb from the effort.

I'll make it, I know I will.

I hang onto my poles for dear life. I move like a snowplow down a mountain road, keeping my eyes dead ahead so I won't be tempted by the precipice. Sweat runs down my skin and makes my clothes heavy. I must not stop. My body heat would disappear in a second and I would not be able to fend off the cold.

I must be halfway there. The wind tears at my coat. I try to make out the shape of the house at the top of the hill. But it is too dark now, and the snow is blinding.

I push forward, concentrating on the cold air rushing into my lungs. With each step my wounds could open. And then as I shift my weight, thinking of the comforting immobility of my splints, my left leg gives way and I collapse.

Face to the ground. When I try to lift myself with my arms, my hands sink into the snow. The wind whirls above me with great gesticulations and its gusts punish my face. I look toward the top of the hill. The snow is falling faster. The house must be there, somewhere, in the maw of winter.

I manage to stand, but I have to attach one of my snowshoes. The cold bites at my fingers and tries to devour my hands. The snow sticks to my clothes, my beard, my eyelashes. The upward slope has disappeared in the darkness.

I breathe deeply, concentrate my energy, and put one foot in front of the other.

But my leg gives way again.

I close my eyes for a moment. When I reach the house, I will get undressed and bundle up in a big wool blanket. A fire will be burning in the fireplace. Matthias will put the soup on. Maybe there will be black bread. I will eat everything he sets down in front of me, then I'll fall asleep, watched over by the light and heat of the flames.

I open my eyes: I am still lying on the ground. And it's snowing like crazy. I roll over, I struggle, I try to get up. But I only sink deeper. The cold is holding me down. Every movement weighs a tonne and I have no more strength. My leg has stopped sending pain signals. I don't feel it anymore. I should have taken shelter with Jonas in the stable. I would have been comfortable in the straw. I would have been warm.

Ice is forming knots on my coat and hat and gloves. I must not stop, I must get up. I'm almost there. I stir into action. Propping myself up on my elbows, I crawl, I twist, I drag myself along the snow. I make a little progress, though it feels like I am sinking. Pulled down by icy underground currents.

I move more and more slowly. My hands are completely numb. Maybe I should do like Matthias and pray.

The blizzard howls. It is impatient, eager to cover me up, embrace me, and close over me. It can salivate a little before it devours me.

I curl up to keep warm. I am like everybody else. I cannot accept the possibility of my death. I am too afraid.

I try to stay calm, but my breathing is out of control.

I can't stay here. I have to keep moving.

The snow is a bed of cutting crystals.

I have to stand up, but the cold won't let me.

I refuse to go this way, bent into myself, face to the ground.

I gather my courage and roll onto my back, my arms outstretched, palms open to the sky.

All around me shadows prowl.

The night is hungry. And the snow carnivorous.

VI. ICARUS

High above, all will be clearer, all will be more
beautiful, and finally I will give myself over to
the light. Finally I will be delivered of wisdom,
measure, and duty. And meanwhile, my son, you
will flap your wings. Later, much later, you will
turn and look behind. No doubt your heart will
freeze in your chest. You will look everywhere,
but you will not find me.

I awake suddenly as if someone had grabbed me by the collar to save me from drowning. I am lying by the fireplace. I feel the weight of my legs at the far end of my body but do not dare move them.

The daylight is dazzling on the other side of the window. The sun is melting the snow on the roof, and water comes streaming down everywhere, along the roofline. The smell of flour is in the air. I turn my head and see Matthias kneeling in front of the fire. On the coals there is a kettle of soup and an aluminum plate with slices of black bread.

I sit up and touch my face. Frostbite has formed a film of dead skin like a snake that has molted.

Matthias looks in my direction. I raise my chin to swallow my saliva. We consider each other for a moment. Then he shakes his head and sighs, disapproving of my stubborn nature. Or refusing to believe in my resilience. I lift my eyebrows. He gives me a bowl of soup and a slice of bread. It has been a while. I eat hungrily. After the meal, Matthias makes instant coffee.

In the village, he says, I found a bag of food on a front porch. I figure someone left it for us. At least that's what I thought when I saw there was a little bit of everything inside. Maybe people aren't so stingy as we thought.

Next to the fireplace is a crowbar and a pile of short planks.

I started pulling up the hardwood floors in the rooms upstairs, he explains. Look how good it burns.

He throws a few pieces on the fire. The varnish melts, bubbles, colouring the flames, then evaporates. The wood is dense. It burns well and produces a lot of heat.

We'll survive this, he predicts, showing me the book that was on his bedside table. The blackout, your accident, this village – just detours, unfinished stories, fortuitous meetings. Winter nights and travellers.

I watch the pieces of wood being consumed. The nails that are left turn red, fall, and are lost in the carpet of hot ashes where the coals glow.

I didn't break anything. My legs are swollen, but I'll be all right. I'll be back walking again, tomorrow, soon. But I probably won't be able to trust them.

Matthias stares at me, his head to one side.

I told you you'd never make it.

We have had a week of good weather, maybe more. At midday, we can feel the temperature rise above the freezing point. But when the sun sets, the landscape drops down below zero as if the illusions of the day had no effect on the world of the night.

Slowly, the skin of my face is healing. I went to look at my reflection in the bathroom mirror, and I just look like I have a bad sunburn.

Yesterday we did an inventory of our reserves. We have been rationing for a while, and skipping a meal now and again. Matthias went to the village this morning. I used the time to do the exercises he taught me earlier in the winter. I concentrated on my leg. So it won't give out on me again in the middle of nowhere.

Early in the afternoon, I stick my nose outside for the first time since Matthias found me in the blizzard. I lean on the door frame and watch the light nestle in the black arms of the trees. With the growing warmth, the snow seems to be sinking deeper into the landscape. I stand there for a time, between the day's warm caresses and the wind's icy hands. I think of my uncles, who must have put out chairs on the front steps of the hunting camp to soak up the sun and listen to the promises spring makes. I think of my map in the wreckage of the porch. And my slingshot and spyglass.

The sight of Matthias climbing the hill tears me from my daydreams. He joins me in the doorway.

I searched a few houses but didn't find much, except for these dried dates. We're not the only ones going over the places with a fine-toothed comb. And this time no one left us any bags of food. I'm going back tomorrow. There are still some houses to check.

We eat a few dates. They are stiff and dry.

With a few of these, he points out, the men of the desert could survive for weeks.

I give him a penetrating look.

How long in the frozen desert?

Eat and we'll see.

We suck the remaining nourishment from the pits and watch the sun flood over the surroundings. I gaze at the distant mountains, a series of superimposed planes.

Suddenly an idea comes to me.

There's a lake in the back country, a few kilometres from here.

What about it?

We can go fishing.

It's winter, he says stubbornly.

I know. And we have everything we need in the basement. A shovel, a chainsaw, fishing line.

Matthias squints at me.

Is it far?

A few kilometres, the other way from the village.

You'll never make it, he tells me categorically.

I'm better and you know it. I'm still limping, but I'm better. We'll leave early to be back before dark.

We move across the crusty snow hardened by the cold of the night. We make slow progress, slowly but surely. Matthias is pulling the sled with the equipment. He is huffing and puffing like an old horse, but he isn't letting go. I'm saving my strength by putting most of my weight on my poles.

When we finally reach the lake, the sun is just peeking over the treetops. We get right to work, moving onto the middle of the frozen surface, then shovelling aside the snow for a few metres in all directions. Beneath our feet the ice is smooth and dark. I start up the chainsaw and cut a wide rectangle. The ice is very thick. It takes a while before the water begins to bubble up and we can push the block under the surface.

I attach gold-coloured lures to the end of our fishing lines. It's not ideal, but it's all I could find. Once we catch something, we will be able to use it for bait. Fish don't have any taboos.

We sit down on the sled. The sun caresses our shoulders and the backs of our heads. Our lines are deep in the cold, black water. From time to time the ice grumbles, and cracks run between our legs and dart across the frozen lake.

The light changes quickly, the sun turns and lengthens our shadows. A snowy owl flies high above without a sound. In its claws it grasps the body of a rabbit that it is about to devour.

Matthias leans over the hole we have cut.

They aren't biting, he sighs. Maybe we should have set snares for rabbits. Do you know how to do that?

My uncles trapped when I was young, but I never tried.

Just then I spot a house hidden among the trees at the edge of the lake. I'm surprised I didn't notice it sooner. From here I can't tell if anyone is living there, but there are no signs of life around it. Once again I could use my spyglass. One thing is clear: there is no smoke coming from the chimney.

Did you see that? I ask Matthias, pointing at the house.

He pays me no mind. He is concentrating on opening a bottle of wine with a corkscrew.

That's the wine Joseph gave us?

Yes, monsieur.

Warmed by the heat of the sun, we drink and stare at our fishing lines. Warmed by the wine too. As we pass the bottle, the air grows milder. There is not a breath of wind. The mountains thrust out their chests, and the snow is splendid.

Tell me, he asks abruptly, do you think that eight canisters of gas is enough?

I glance at the house by the shore. Nothing moving there. But if there are people inside, they must be watching. And laughing because we haven't caught anything.

What do you think? Matthias insists.

It depends.

He nods and waits for the rest.

It depends on the motor, it depends on the road, it depends on all kinds of things.

But it's possible?

I consider the sun that has started its descent toward the horizon.

Yes, maybe. With a little luck.

He gets to his feet, shouting.

I've got something, I've got a bite!

He reels in his line, as excited as a schoolboy, and pulls a handsome trout from the dark waters of the lake. With one hand he proudly displays his catch. With the other he grabs the bottle of wine. He keeps the pose a moment as if I were going to take a picture, then sits down silently, watching the life slip away from the fish's writhing form.

Give it to me, I tell him.

I unhook the trout and cut it into pieces so we can bait our hooks. As soon as we get our lines back in the water, Matthias pulls another trout to the surface. Two minutes later it's my turn to get lucky.

We're off to the races.

And we still have plenty of wine.

For three days, we ate all the fish we could. Today we are smoking the rest. A cloud is floating through the living room. Our eyes are stinging and our clothes stink.

We set the fillets on a grill above the fire and feed it slowly, just enough to keep it from going out. That way the smoke stays dense and thick. It is easy, but it takes forever. It shouldn't cook, it should dry. Matthias made that clear.

If there's any water left in the meat, it will rot.

For hours and hours, heads spinning from the smoke, we watch, hypnotized by the glowing embers and the delightful perspective of meals to come.

ONE HUNDRED FIFTY-NINE

For some time now, we have not had to take turns keeping an eye on the fire. The cold is still insistent, but during the day, the heat of the sun helps us keep the house warm. From time to time, blocks of ice break off from the roof, slide down, and crash to the ground. Each time a powerful groan shakes the walls and we jump, as if an avalanche were bearing down on us. The ice that falls from the roof piles up in front of the window, the doorway, all around the house. It is surrounding us, walling us in.

This morning, opening my eyes, I hear an unusual sound. For a moment I figure another piece of icy snow is falling from the roof, and then I think someone is trying to sneak into the house. But the sound is coming from the chimney. Carefully, I approach the fireplace and stick my head into its black mouth. Suddenly, something bursts from the darkness and pushes against my face. I try to protect myself and end up falling backward. Matthias wakes up, startled at seeing me in a cloud of soot and ashes.

Above our heads a bird is frenetically throwing itself against the ceiling and windows. We want to capture it, but it is quick and frightened. Matthias throws his coat over it like a net and manages to still its flight. I take it firmly in my hands. It is a beautiful thing. Its heart is beating like crazy. At the same time it is completely calm. As if ready to die.

Outside, I ease my grip. For a fraction of a second the bird is motionless. Then it flies off and disappears.

We stand on the porch, as if waiting for something. The day is dawning before us and the snow gauge is standing free. Finally we go inside because of the morning chill.

I make coffee and contemplate the living room. We have taken apart the floor, done our washing, and darned our clothes. And stuffed ourselves on smoked fish. As we do every day, at every meal.

Matthias goes to the window and gazes pensively outside.

We could have varied our menu and eaten that bird, he points out.

True, I agree.

A little later Matthias heads off to the village in search of food. He looks determined. When he closes the door, a block of snow slides off the roof. I hear it pick up speed and crash to the ground with a dull, heavy thud. Just behind Matthias who goes on his way as if nothing had happened.

Matthias returns from the village at the end of the afternoon. I spot him coming up the slope. He is walking head down, and his progress is laborious. With every step his snowshoes sink into the wet snow. He comes in and collapses onto the sofa without taking off his boots.

His clothes are spattered with blood.

I found something to eat, he explains. But it didn't go the way I thought it would.

I do nothing. I say nothing. I can't keep my eyes off from the blood on his coat and pants.

Heat some water, he asks, barely lifting his head, do you mind? I have to wash off.

I stoke the fire and fill two kettles with snow. Matthias lets his clothes drop to the floor and wraps himself in a blanket. I ask no questions. I pick up his clothing and put it in the wash basin. A revolver slips to the floor. He bends over, picks it up, and hides it under the sofa cushions, away from my prying eyes.

I'd spotted a house that didn't seem to have had any visitors for a while. Right behind the church. Maybe I could get my hands on something. Even if it was only some ketchup and mustard. People always leave stuff behind. I was trying to force the door when Jonas came up behind me in a panic. At first I thought he wanted pemmican, but he told me he needed help, he was being threatened. I showed him the house I was trying to break into, and told him he'd be better off hiding, but he wouldn't hear of it. I had to go with him. I followed him to the stable. Five people were standing by the door. Four men and a woman.

They want to kill, they want to kill one of my cows, Jonas explained to me. He was a nervous wreck. They want to kill one of my cows. There's only three left, just three.

I went over to the little group and we talked. It was very simple. They were starving. And there were three cows in the stable.

Jonas was desperate, but he knew he couldn't stop the group. I asked him why he had come looking for me.

No one said anything.

I hear you have a gun, one of the men finally said.

I denied it.

That's not what Jonas told us, he replied. Listen, nobody's got a gun here anymore. Jude and his bunch took them all. We looked everywhere.

I started to back away.

We just want you to shoot a cow, the lady begged. We'll share the meat.

It's true, Jonas said. That's why I went looking for you. The last time, the other time you went looking through your things to give me a piece of pemmican, I saw your gun, I saw your gun under your belt.

Why don't you use a knife? I asked.

They're my cows, Jonas insisted, they're my cows. I don't want them to suffer. I don't want them to panic. The last time, the last time it turned out badly. Me, I told them to wait when I saw you go by.

I nodded my head.

Thank you, Jonas murmured, relieved, thank you.

It all happened very fast.

We went into the stable. They pointed out the cow. It was

tied to a post. I took out my gun. The cow was beautiful and very calm. I walked right up to it, put the barrel of the gun to its ear, and fired. I didn't think it would go off that quickly. And that the explosion would be so loud. The cow stood there a moment, then slid slowly to the ground. I don't know why, but I wanted to catch it in its fall. But it was too heavy. I nearly broke my back. The next thing I knew, the guys started to cut up the animal. I let them go about their business, and I went back outside where Jonas was.

When he saw me, his eyes got wide and he looked away.

What's wrong?

Blood, the blood on your clothes, he told me.

When I saw what had happened to my coat, my head started spinning.

Matthias is quiet. I look at him. His shoulders slump forward, his face is thin, his eyes are surrounded by dark circles. Suddenly he looks like nothing. Nothing but a weary body worn by years and circumstances.

During the great wars, he tells me, when the army was retreating, soldiers ate horses. Here it's the end of the winter, and we're eating our cows.

I take out the piece of meat he brought. It's a good cut. I slice off several pieces and fry them quickly in a pan. When it is ready, I offer him dinner.

No thanks, I'm not hungry.

The ceiling is low. The clouds are sewn to the snow. It has been raining for the last ten days. Sometimes hard, sometimes just drizzle. As if the skies wanted to speed things up now and melt the landscape.

We tear down the room dividers and closets upstairs to feed the fireplace and bring down the humidity. When we pull off the drywall, dust goes billowing through the rooms and galaxies of particles float in the grey light of day. With a sledgehammer we break down the uprights, the lintels, and the two-by-fours. With every blow the house echoes like an empty theatre. Then we saw everything into pieces. A lot of work for not much wood. But it keeps us busy.

Often, before breaking down some sections, we have to cut the electrical wires that run from one wall to the next. I think of radiators, switches, ceiling lamps. I think of the constellations of green and red indicators that belong to electrical equipment. All that seems light years away.

During the day, we take long breaks and go to the window to watch nature's slow transformation.

Winter's finishing up, Matthias says pensively, several times over. The roads will be passable soon enough.

Every time he mentions his departure, I wonder what kind of

condition the city is in. Maybe power has been re-established, and life is going back to normal. Or maybe everyone has fled, abandoning the old, the sick, and the weak. Like here.

EIGHTY-NINE

The temperature fell below freezing today. The snow hardened in the cold air, and we can walk on it a lot more easily. We use the opportunity to go in search of provisions.

To increase our chances, we split up. Matthias goes to the village, of course, and I climb toward the house by the lake.

As I close in on it, I look across to the mountains. I can feel the trees wanting to shake off the snow. There are no footprints around the house. The place looks deserted. No one has shovelled around the front door. I don't know why, but the old shed attracts my attention. As if work spaces and storerooms have always been more familiar than the order and comfort of the house.

I want to go in, but the doors are caught in the snow and ice. I break a small window around the side. I make sure to break the glass cleanly, then I climb through.

The inside of the shed smells of dust, old oil, and closed-in spaces. My eyes grow accustomed and, little by little, the darkness gives up its secrets. Wood shavings, tools, tobacco cans full of screws, nails, and bolts. A wide workbench runs along the wall. At the back, by a heap of shovels and rakes, I spot two gas cans. There is even a canoe, upside down, in the rafters.

In the middle a tarp covers a heavy-looking block. I lift the cloth: it's a four-by-four ATV. An old model. I sit down on the seat and put my hands on the controls. As I rest my leg, I picture myself speeding down the logging roads.

The key is in the ignition. I turn it. No answer. The battery must be dead. I pull on the starter rope. Nothing doing there either. I look beneath the machine to inspect the starter cable. Everything seems to be in working order. I take off the spark plug and carburetor, then clean and replace them.

I get back up and feel that this time the machine will roar to life. I pull on the rope and the motor starts right up. I hit the accelerator to wake up the engine. The smell of combustion fills the shed. When I turn it off and replace the tarp, I think of Matthias with his car and figure that I have no reason to envy him.

On the way out, I cover the window with a piece of plywood. It is still light out, but the day will soon be over. If I want to get back by nightfall, I won't have time to look through the house. That will wait.

On the way home, I turn around a few times. I'm worried. The shed is a treasure chest, and even if the snow is hard, my tracks can still be seen. Anyone could follow them. You can't hide anything from the snow.

FIFTY-THREE

The snow has melted by half over the last few days. Or nearly half. Enough so we can make out the rushing veins of water running beneath what remains of the ice and snow. When we step onto the porch and listen, we can hear the rivulets. In spots we can see bare ground. Islands of yellow grass, crushed by winter. When we turn our eyes toward the village, we see that sections of the road are starting to appear where the sun shines with full force.

It is evening now. Sitting across from each other, we are eating a can of corn beef that Matthias managed to unearth during his last expedition. We each take a spoonful, alternating scrupulously. When we have finished, he throws the metal container into the fire. The label burns immediately, then the metal glows red before turning completely black.

I did not tell Matthias what I discovered in the shed. He reveals none of his preparations, though he does describe the book he is reading, where the inhabitants of a village set in the middle of the jungle have been held prisoner by solitude for the last hundred years.

Matthias blows out the candle and we settle in to sleep. We stare at the ceiling weakly lit by the shimmering glow of the embers. Then he tells me he would have liked to play a game of chess. I warn him that I would have beaten him. We laugh.

And I say I would have gladly drunk another bottle of wine. Like that day on the lake.

His voice is so low I can scarcely hear him when he says that was one of the best times all winter.

In the fireplace the ashes have won over the embers. The darkness is complete, and the silence that settles over us is comfortable.

FORTY-EIGHT

I open my eyes when I hear the door close. Outside it is light, but the sun hasn't risen yet. The fire has been lit and the coffee is ready. I go to the window with a blanket wrapped around my shoulders. Matthias is heading down the hill.

Something isn't right. Why would he go to the village this early? I'm confused. Then I see the note on the bedside table. I don't bother reading it, I pull on my clothes and rush outside. When he hears me calling, he stops and looks back. I reach him, limping and out of breath.

What's with you?

Where are you going?

To the village – why?

There's still too much snow, I tell him.

Matthias sighs, then looks me over. As if nothing ever happens the way he'd planned.

Look at me, look around, he tells me, furious. I'm old, I was patient all winter, and now spring is here. I can't wait anymore. I've waited too much as it is. The roads are passable, the snow is melting fast. Look, you can see the asphalt on the village streets.

There's still too much snow, I'm telling you, you'll get stuck.

I've got a car, gas, tires with chains, and food. I even have a gun.

That's not the point. Wait a few more days. Until it melts some more.

I'm the one who's melting. I can't take it anymore. I took care of you, you're fine now, so let me go. I need to get back to my wife, can't you understand? I need to find her.

I take a step closer, hoping to reason with him. Matthias backs away.

Let me at least walk you to the village.

No, he shouts. You're going to turn around and leave me alone.

I move closer to him.

There's too much snow, I insist, the roads will be blocked when you get to the mountains, you won't even reach the villages on the coast.

Just as I'm about to put my hand on his shoulder, he pushes me away and pulls out his gun.

I freeze. His hand is trembling.

Above our heads a flight of geese crosses the sky, squawking.

You're going to turn around, Matthias repeats. And you're going to let me go.

He moves away, backing off carefully, the gun still pointed at me. The sun is rising. The geese have passed. I can hear them, though they have disappeared from sight. Matthias turns and disappears, following the slope down to the village. I know he would not have fired, but I didn't want to push things.

FORTY-SIX

Back at the house, I pace for a while. I drop onto the sofa and close my eyes, but sleep does not come. The smell of rotting fish hangs in the room. With all the humidity, the last bits have started to rot. I hurry outside to throw them away, then circle the house, looking for something to do. I stand in front of the fleshless body of the porch, which has become visible with the melting snow. Several times, I hear a car engine in the distance, down the hill.

I make my way through the debris and icy snow. I can't get all the way to the trap door to the cellar, but by lifting lengths of sheet metal and planks, I find several dented cans, a torn bag of noodles, and a few damp packets of powdered soup. Everything is in bad shape, and I don't know whether I'll be able to do anything with it.

By using a plank as a lever, I manage to lift part of the collapsed roof. Carefully, I crawl on my belly through the opening I have made. It is like a cave, an underground chamber spared by the snow. I move forward, feeling my way, and come upon my slingshot and, a little further on, my spyglass. I slip on some wet paper. It is the map Joseph gave me. I take hold of it, move out of the wreckage again, and go back to the living room.

The map is drying by the fire. It was damaged by water, but

no information was lost. Over and over, with the tip of my index finger, I retrace the route that leads to my uncles' hunting camp.

The fire burns down. I throw on a few more planks, and the flames illuminate the room again. I gaze at the objects I brought back, relics like the tin cans, and next to them the strips of bark on the floor. I pick up the note Matthias left. Three lines of black ink.

We survived the winter. I'll never forget it. Now it's time to leave. The next step can't wait and you know it. Farewell.

I put the scrap of paper in my pocket and suddenly feel very alone. Matthias is right. Winter is finishing up. There's nothing more to do here.

THIRTY-NINE

I can't sleep at night. I think of Matthias journeying toward the city with his supplies and his gun. I think of Joseph and Maria, happy somewhere, far from the village. And my aunts and uncles watching the fast-flowing river and playing cards. I think of the ATV waiting for me in the shed.

I get up as soon as I spot the first glow of dawn through the window. I slip the spyglass, slingshot, Joseph's map, and my meagre provisions into the pockets of my coat, then step outside, closing the door securely behind me.

The next step can't wait. It's true. It's my turn to leave.

The sky is grey and smooth. Like a blanket draped over the landscape. The snow is heavy and sticky. With every step, I have to clean off my snowshoes with my poles to make any progress.

I reach the house by the lake. There are no fresh tracks. I am the only one who knows the secrets of this place. With one snowshoe I push aside the snow and ice from the shed doors. A padlock keeps the latch shut, but it is not locked. When I open the doors, the ATV is there, waiting under its tarp.

I sort through the piles of objects and tools in the shed and put everything useful in a box and strap it to the front of the ATV. A sleeping bag, a hammer, a short saw, a retractable knife, rope, and the tarp. All sorts of things. Among the treasures is an old pack of cigarettes. There are six left. I finish the job: I tie the gas cans on the back, on the luggage carrier, and I walk down to the lake with a cigarette in my mouth.

The ice is covered by a good layer of water. The lake is about to break up. Its surface is grey and featureless. Like the sky. I can't tell where the lake begins and the shoreline ends.

I move a little closer and light my cigarette.

The mountains rise up around the lake and close one upon the other. I squint and make out a path that leads into the back country. A white line on a white background. That must be the way to go. There is always a lot of snow in the woods at the end of winter. If I bog down, I can use the ATV's winch to get unstuck. Those machines are made to get through anything.

My cigarette is very good, and I smoke it down to the filter. I throw the butt toward the lake and turn around to head back to the shed. But when I move, the snow gives way beneath my feet and I'm up to my thighs in water. My boots and clothes are soaked in a matter of seconds. I try to get free, but I have nothing to hold onto, and the ice breaks when I put any weight on it. I finally manage to drag myself back onto the snow by stretching out full length. But once I start crawling, the surface opens up again and I fall back into the icy water. By the time I reach the shore, I am frozen stiff. It's not easy finding my feet. My clothes weigh a tonne and I have lost my sense of direction. I have lost my coordination, too, and I have to concentrate to put one foot in front of the other. I stop in front of the shed. I am trembling, my teeth are chattering, and I am afraid I'm going to pass out with every breath. I need dry clothes. Now. Right now.

I move toward the house. My heart is pounding, but it is barely delivering any blood to my limbs. I throw myself against the door. It is locked. It looks like the downstairs windows have been boarded up from inside. The ones upstairs are out of reach. Cold is taking hold of me a little more firmly with each second. I can't open and close my hands anymore.

I check the door and try to take a deep breath. Use my shoulder. My hip. My feet. The frame splinters, and the door finally gives way. I fall forward inside the house and pull off my clothes as fast as possible, struggling on the floor. The scars on my legs are deep blue. I run upstairs, shivering, open the first chest of drawers I see, and throw on all the clothes I can.

The socks, long johns, pants, wool sweater – they're all a little small for me but that doesn't matter. I sit on the edge of the bed and rub my legs for as long as I can.

When my limbs thaw out, I explore the room. I go to the closet in hopes of finding a pair of boots. When I open the door, my heart stops. Beneath the clothes on hangers is a shadow curled up on itself. It is motionless. I bend over. It is a woman. She is thin and old. Her white hair is shiny, her skin diaphanous, her eyes wide open. In a panic I exit the room and go down the stairs, making as little noise as possible, as if I had disturbed the repose of a very tired person.

Everything is impeccable in her kitchen. The floor is clean, the dishes are stacked in the cupboards, and an immaculate oil lamp stands proudly in the centre of the table. Home-made preserves are carefully lined up in the pantry along with baskets of garlic, onions, and potatoes. Only the cold and the dead plants on the windowsill betray the harmony of the room.

For a moment I wonder why I didn't come here earlier. Matthias and I would have had something to eat, and the lady might have been freed from her loneliness.

In the vestibule I come upon a lumberjack shirt and rain boots. They will have to do. I pick supplies at random, gather up my wet clothes, and go out, trying to close the smashed-in door as best I can. Then, slowly, very slowly, I go back, regretting that I have to put off my departure. But as I walk away, I am not thinking so much of my aunts and uncles in their hunting camp but of the distress of the old woman in her closet.

THIRTY-THREE

When I make it back to the house at the end of the afternoon, the birds are pecking away at the rotten fish. I stop to watch them, then go into the living room. And here I thought I would never set foot in this place again. I try stoking the fire, but there is no more wood, and I don't have the strength to attack the kitchen walls. Nor to go outside and gather wet branches.

At one spot in the room are the books we piled up when we burned the shelves. The books where Matthias poached his stories. I lean over and grab a few of them, the first ones I get to. I go back to the fireplace and, without hesitation, throw one onto the embers. The cover catches almost immediately. The corners roll up and the cardboard bends in the flames. The first pages bunch into each other. The book opens like an accordion. The heat is intense, but soon the book is no more than a shapeless, orange-and-black mass. Like a fragile, burning stone. I throw another book on, and the flames leap higher, spiralling up the chimney, and bright light fills the room. I take off all my clothes to enjoy the heat of the books and eat a few pickled beets from the old woman's house. As I watch the pages burn, I wonder where Matthias might be about now. Further than I've gotten, that's for sure.

Suddenly I hear the door creak. Someone has entered the house. It is a reflex: I tie a blanket around my waist and pick up the poker. The footsteps come down the hallway. I hide against the wall. Maybe it is the ghost of the old woman coming to reclaim her beets. A figure stops in the doorway. I stand motionless, both hands gripping the poker. The intruder must be on his guard too. I hold my breath. Then Matthias walks into the room. When he spots me in the corner, he looks surprised. It must be what I'm wearing. We size each other up a moment, then he begins coughing uncontrollably.

I lost control of the car, he explains, disoriented and still in a state of panic. In the curve before the big hill, a few kilometres past the village. I wasn't going fast, but I skidded into the ditch. The snow ... the snow took my car. I couldn't do anything about it. I had to walk to get back here. It's over now, everything is over.

I hand him the jar of beets. He eats a few, his eyes empty.

I left everything back there. His voice is trembling. My stuff, the supplies, the gas.

You're exhausted, I tell him, throwing a few books on the fire. You need to sleep. We'll see what we can do tomorrow.

I'm afraid. I'm afraid of being stuck here, he sobs, lying down on the sofa.

It is cold in the living room this morning. Matthias is still asleep. His white hair is stuck to his forehead. His beard is dirty and his closed eyes are sunk deep in their sockets.

As I stir the ashes to awaken the embers, I see there are bits of paper where a few words, a part of a sentence, are still legible. As if Matthias's return had frozen the flames.

I go out for some fresh air. It is snowing. The snowflakes are tiny, like confetti. I consider Matthias's stubbornness, his misfortune, as I watch the birds pecking away at the remains of the fish. Some of them hop from piece to piece, others concentrate on a single prize, but all of them are agitated and on the alert. When I go inside to get my slingshot, they fly off in a disorderly cloud. And when I go back onto the porch, a few minutes later, they return, one by one.

I wonder what it must be like to have lived as long as Matthias has. And shared your whole life with the same woman. Be afraid you might lose her. And die alone, by yourself. Like the old woman in the house by the lake.

The harsh cry of blue jays stirs me from my thoughts. Several of the birds are perched on.an electric wire. One of them spreads its wings, flies past the house, and lands on the snow, a few steps from the porch. It evaluates its chances with its piercing, intelligent eyes, then moves toward the fish, its head cocked. Slowly, I raise my arm, pull back the elastic, and aim. I let fly with a shot. The projectile whips past it, over its head, and disappears into the snow without a sound. The bird lifts its head, but does not move. I wait a little, then try another shot. This time, the bird topples over backward. When I go to pick it up, its wings are still quivering with the final reflexes of its nervous system. I take up position again and wait for another bird of its size to land in front of me, guided by its stomach and the light of spring.

Matthias wakes up as I am making our meal. He seems to be in better shape. Sleep has restored his energy. He sips at a glass of warm water, then takes out the one book he had brought along with him in his coat pocket.

This book is precious, he tells me. I've read you a few passages from it.

A good thing he carried it with him. Otherwise I would have thrown it in the fire with the other ones to cook our food.

Listen, he begins, setting the book on his lap, and take heed. A man had two sons. One day, the youngest announced to his father that he was leaving. Fine, said the father, I will give you half of what I possess, for the other half will go to your brother. Not long after, having gathered together the fortune, the youngest son went off to a faraway country and dissipated everything in debauchery. When all was spent, he found himself empty-handed and was forced to feed the pigs that belonged to a rich land-owner. To quell his hunger, he was ready to dip into the animals' feed, but that was forbidden. In desperation, he decided to run away. Though he no longer considered himself the worthy son of his father, he returned to his homeland. He approached the house, feeling ashamed and lost, and when his father saw him, he threw his arms around him. I am not worthy to be your son, the young man said. But the father ordered a fatted calf to be slaughtered and a great banquet to be held for his glorious return. Let us eat and make merry, he sang, for my son was dead and now he has returned to life, he was lost and now he is found. During the festivities the eldest son came back from the fields. He questioned the guests and learned that a fatted calf had been killed to celebrate his brother's return. When he saw his father, the eldest flew into a rage. All these years I have worked for you without a word of complaint, he spoke, and you never as much as gave me a goat kid that I might feast with my friends. And now your youngest son returns after wasting half your fortune, and you kill a fatted calf. The father looked at his son. Then he answered in a soft voice. My son, you are always by my side and everything I have is yours. But we had to hold a feast and make merry because your brother was dead and now he has returned to life, he was lost and now he is found.

I motion to Matthias to sit down. The meal is ready. He sits near the fireplace, stares at his plate, then looks up.

What is this?

It's the feast.

We begin to eat. The flesh is tough. We have to chew every mouthful at length.

Matthias picks up a piece and holds it up, examining it.

This meat's like leather. What is it?

Blue jay.

Oh, he says, turning toward the books I have piled next to the fireplace.

We finish our plates without further conversation.

TWENTY-NINE

After we eat I tell Matthias to get dressed and come with me.

He doesn't react.

I insist.

Come on, I need your help. Take everything you need, we won't be coming back.

He finally gets a move on, and we start out for the house by the lake. When we reach the shed, I ask him to wait for me. He stands there, frozen to the spot, while I get two shovels.

We go to the edge of the forest and I start digging a hole in the snow at the foot of a tree. At first Matthias just watches me, then he picks up a shovel. When we hit the ground, we try to keep digging, but it is as hard as a rock.

That's good enough, I say, and ask him to come with me.

We leave the shovels behind and go into the house. When we walk through the kitchen on our way to the stairs, Matthias notices how orderly everything is.

It's so clean here, he murmurs, as if astonished. Everything in its place.

We go upstairs to the woman's room.

When we come to the closet, Matthias jumps. It is his turn to look like a ghost.

You take her legs and I'll take her arms.

He leans over the woman and looks at her, then caresses her forehead with the back of his hand.

All right, he says, finally, after closing her eyes, let's go.

The cold has preserved the woman's corpse. She is as stiff and hard as stone. We can't loosen her limbs. To carry her we have to wrap her in a sheet. She is so rigid and so light she seems to weigh nothing. We take her to the edge of the forest without too much effort and place her gently in the hole.

She could be my wife, Matthias says, looking at her body in the grave.

Then we grab the shovels and cover her with a thick layer of snow.

Matthias goes back to the house and returns with the oil lamp that was on the kitchen table. He lights it and sets it like a votive candle at the foot of the tree.

Come on, I tell him, come with me, we're not finished.

Wait, he whispers, staring at the flame wavering in its chimney.

Then he crosses himself, kisses the mound of snow, and falls in behind me.

TWENTY-EIGHT

We are by the shed now. As I open the doors, Matthias spots my tracks that lead toward the lake and disappear into the water.

You almost didn't make it, he says.

The water is cold as ice.

We go into the little building. The ATV is there, loaded and ready to go. I take off the case I attached in front, and motion to Matthias to sit down at the controls. He refuses. He has never driven a vehicle like this, but I insist and he ends up agreeing.

You'll be able to go everywhere with this thing.

He looks at me, unsure what I mean.

You'll be able to leave the village, no problem. Just go and get your things from the car.

The light of hope gleams in his eyes.

You'll see, this machine hardly uses any gas at all. You can make it to the city with what you have.

Matthias's look of gratitude is so strong, it shakes me.

Thank you. Oh, thank you so much.

You'll be careful on the road, okay? Don't drive too fast, and don't stay too long in one place. And avoid the checkpoints.

I'll be all right, he promises, showing me the revolver in his belt.

I tell him how the starter cord works. Matthias pulls on it, and after eight or ten tries, the engine starts backfiring. Shouting over the racket, I quickly explain how the clutch works, and the winch, and the handbrake.

The next minute he is hugging me and kissing me on the forehead, then he pulls away, leaving deep tracks behind. I wave goodbye, but I don't think he sees me.

A mild breeze blows through the forest. The sun is beating down. The landscape is made of running water and the snow looks like big kernels of corn, scattered with pine needles, branches, and dead leaves.

Before disappearing altogether, Matthias turns around, waves one quick hand in the air, and nervously grabs the controls again. As if he were riding a bucking bronco.

I sit down heavily in the snow. I feel happy, and worried too. For Matthias and for myself.

VII. SUN

Your heart will surely freeze in your chest. You will look for me everywhere, but you will not find me. You will see only a few feathers blowing in the sunlight. Then, and only then, it will be your turn to be free, you will go on your way with no concern for me.

ELEVEN

It is the new moon tonight. The stars pierce the darkness with dazzling precision. From time to time, the green-tinted northern lights illuminate part of the sky.

Sometimes, when the sky is cloudy, I hear thunder in the distance. As if spring were demanding to be let in. When I look carefully at the trees, I can see the buds are full of sap, ready to burst open.

My leg is doing better. I am still limping, but it's better. Leaning on my poles, I can walk as long·as I need to. Maria would be happy.

Since Matthias left I sleep here and there, exploring the abandoned houses in the village. I live off the provisions from the old woman's house and a few unexpected discoveries.

All that is left now are heaps of icy, dirty snow, and everywhere are the ruins of winter. Wrecked cars in the streets, the yards, at the edge of the fields. Sagging structures, bent lamp posts, and uprooted trees.

The village is unrecognizable. And almost deserted. A few small groups of people move from place to place in search of food and fuel. Wary packs of skeletal coyotes.

One morning Jonas comes up to me.

Beautiful day, he declares, his arms flying in every direction. Warm day, the bears, the bears are going to come out of their dens soon. Did you see? Did you see the level and the colour of the river? Long trees, there are long trees as long as the steeple uprooted by the current. Some are even rubbing under the bridge. And then me, I don't know what to do, what to do with my cows. I know they want to slaughter them, slaughter them soon, I know everybody's starting to get hungry, everybody's always hungry now. So I untied them so they'll run away, so they'll disappear. They went out of the stable, but they didn't go far. I tried, I tried to scare them. That didn't work either. It's like they don't want to leave. By the way if you see Matthias, tell him, tell him I'm ready to go sell my bottles. I've got a lot, and that's going to add up to a lot, a lot of money.

Jonas stares into my face, then jams his hand into his turquoise coat and comes up with a slab of pemmican.

Here, he tells me in a confidential tone, you'll see, it's a little hard, but it's very good. You'll see.

He tells me to look for shelter because it's going to rain, then he disappears.

He is right. It starts to rain right after he leaves. I look over my itinerary on the map. I figure it will take me fifteen days with the condition my leg is in. If all goes well. One last time I sort through my supplies, count out my provisions, and pack my bag. I fall asleep thinking how surprised my aunts and uncles are going to be when I walk into their camp.

SEVEN

The rain stopped during the night. Dawn has just laid its hand on the horizon.

I walk quickly through the village. When I reach the garage, I stop a minute. I have not set foot there ever since. If I open the door, will I see my father, working underneath a car? I hesitate, look around, then keep walking.

At the top of the hill, I pause in front of the house where Matthias and I spent the winter. My legs are fine, but my pack is heavy and I have to catch my breath. The porch looks like a battlefield. Further on, in the clearing, the snow gauge has fallen over.

The ground is spongy and the young ferns are feeding off last autumn's dead grass. I lift my head. Before me the tall spruce stand straight and black. They mark the end of the village and the beginning of the forest.

ACKNOWLEDGMENTS

The author would like to thank Mylène Bouchard, Brigitte Caron, Nicolas Rochette, Laurence Grandbois-Bernard, Aimée Verret, Michel Guay, Nicolas Grenier, Micheline Bérubé, and Jean-Marc Desroches, as well as the Canada Council for the Arts for its financial support.

DAVID HOMEL is the author of twelve novels. As a translator, he has twice won the Governor General's Award. He lives in Montreal.

PHOTO BY MARINA VULICEVIC

CHRISTIAN GUAY-POLIQUIN was born just north of the U.S. border in Saint-Armand, Québec, in 1982. His first novel, *Le fil des kilomètres*, was published by both La Peuplade and Bibliothèque québécoise in Québec, and by Phébus in France. It appeared in English as *Running on Fumes* (Talonbooks, 2016). *The Weight of Snow* is being translated into nine languages (including Spanish, Italian, German, and Czech) and is enjoying great public and critical success in France and Québec.